NIGHT OF THE
ASSHOLES

Also by **Kevin L. Donihe**

Shall We Gather at the Garden?
Ocean of Lard (with Carlton Mellick III)
The Greatest Fucking Moment in Sports
Grape City
House of Houses
Washer Mouth: The Man Who Was a Washing Machine

NIGHT OF THE ASSHOLES

KEVIN L. DONIHE

Eraserhead Press
Portland, OR

This is a work of parody, as defined by the Fair Use Doctrine. Any similarities, without satirical intent, to copyrighted characters, or individuals living or dead, are purely coincidental.

ERASERHEAD PRESS
205 NE BRYANT
PORTLAND, OR 97211

WWW.ERASERHEADPRESS.COM

ISBN: 1-936383-22-5

AUTHOR'S NOTE

This book is a parody of George A. Romero's NIGHT OF THE LIVING DEAD.

You probably figured that out prior to reading this.

Goodbye.

—Kevin L. Donihe
October 10, 2010

CHAPTER ONE

Damn, what an asshole, Barbara thought as the black sedan veered into her lane and nearly scraped paint off the side of her car. The other driver held down his horn, like it was somehow her fault. It seemed to Barbara there were more assholes in the world now than when she was a kid, or even when she was in college.

She considered rolling down her window and shooting the guy a bird. But Barbara didn't want to be just another asshole, acting out of mindless aggression. That had led her to pummel the people in her life—and even strangers—for petty, vindictive, or patently dumb reasons. There was enough pain in the world, she realized. It wasn't her place to bring more of it.

But being trapped in a car with a Hare Krishna, Barbara found it difficult to bury her emotions.

"Hare Krishna Hare Krishna
Krishna Krishna Hare Hare
Hare Rama Hare Rama
Rama Rama Hare Hare," sang the bald, robe-clad man in the passenger's seat.

Barbara muttered. Spots appeared before her eyes, red like her hair. They were familiar to her, the angry spots, or so she'd called them. But she didn't give in to temptation. She didn't punch or kick him. She didn't even scream. Barbara vowed months ago not to lash out at others, and besides, the Hare Krishna was her brother.

Johnny repeated the mantra. Barbara's spots began to dance. She gripped the steering wheel tighter and focused only on the unfurling road. In the past, she rarely attempted restraint, preferring instead to tear into those who angered her, sometimes without recourse or memory of what had transpired. The doctor said the pills would help stop that. They were little and blue and made her feel funny for the first few weeks. But she'd adapted to them. Now, they didn't even make her drowsy, and angry spots flashed more often in shades of gray rather than red.

The pills didn't offer a complete solution, but that was okay. It made her responsible for her own self-improvement. Even without medication, she didn't want to be angry anymore.

But old habits were hard to break, so her doctor had given her a stress doll. It was life-sized, made of rags, sexless and faceless. She could project whoever's features she wanted onto it, and she'd pounded the thing for a solid fifteen minutes before leaving to pick up Johnny. She imagined eyes and poked them. She imagined nuts and kicked them. Ghost teeth met her fist more times than she wanted to count. Barbara would have to sew the doll's head back on and patch its belly before using it again.

It wasn't Johnny she was mad at, just what he'd become. At heart, he was a sweet, good-natured boy. When she was a teenager and he a child, he'd been a calming influence, rarely a bother and fun to be around.

Barbara was almost certain his Hare Krishna phase would pass. Six months before, he'd been a leather-jacketed punk, replete with sneer and Mohawk. A year ago: a dreadlocked Rastafarian. She'd rather liked Rasta-Johnny. He always had weed, and that calmed her almost as much as medication. His Southern Baptist incarnation hadn't been as fruitful, nor had his stint as a clown. But he was just 24 years old, and she could forgive him for not yet knowing who he was or what he wanted to be. She just wished he didn't have to be a Hare Krishna right now.

At the very least, his new outlook had aided their reconciliation. Johnny hadn't spoken to Barbara for months after the Thanksgiving episode with the turkey drumstick and the gravy boat and her brother's new Mohawk. That changed the moment he handed her the first flower. No longer did he mention the past, preferring to smile a lot and stare upwards, sometimes at the sun. When she asked him to accompany her to the mall, he agreed without hesitation.

In truth, she didn't want to go anywhere with her brother. But it was time for a test. She was to meet her mom by the theater later. Before then, she had to spend two hours with Johnny as he sang the mantra, smiled, and handed out pamphlets and flowers.

She did, however, intend to pick up a small insurance policy: one cherry vanilla smoothie, extra large. She ordered it whenever she came to the mall, even when Johnny wasn't around, because it was nostalgic and reminded her of simpler times. Holding a cup would likewise occupy fingers that might otherwise clutch a cigarette.

The mall came into view. Barbara had to believe she wouldn't break, with or without a smoothie. Her doctor had told her she was the fount of change and its engine, that she alone guided her destiny and created her future self. The power was within; she just had to find it.

CHAPTER TWO

Entering the parking lot, Barbara grimaced at the sheer number of cars. She pulled into one of the few empty spots while Johnny scooped up an armful of flowers and tied a sack full of pamphlets around his waist. All were written by A. C. Bhaktivedanta Swami Prabhupada. Though Johnny had said the name quite a few times, Barbara still had no idea how to pronounce it.

Johnny held out a few flowers. "Care to help me spread higher consciousness?"

"No. No thank you."

He nodded. Smiled. He always smiled. Sometimes she wanted to... No, she couldn't think that thought. Instead, Barbara imagined a field full of flowers, but then realized the flowers reminded her of Johnny, so she uprooted them, replaced them with wheat.

Her brother stepped out of the car, and Barbara sat there for a few seconds, bottom lip between her teeth, still thinking of the field.

"You coming?" he asked.

"Yeah. I'm just...getting ready."

He said nothing more, though a smile beamed.

Barbara removed her mind from the field and left the car. She could do this. It would be easy. Johnny was her brother and she loved him, even if he never stopped being a Hare Krishna. Barbara just hoped no one at the mall would get too pissed at him. If one person started shouting, it felt only natural to shout back, which invited others to join the chorus.

Johnny led, and Barbara followed close behind. She wished she could have a cigarette before entering, but wasn't sure how a Hare Krishna might feel about smoking, and hearing Johnny scold her would open the anger window wide.

A few yards ahead, a homeless man stood between a row of cars, sometimes bending over to look into windows, or lifting handles, perhaps to see if doors were locked. His clothes were yellow, brown, and tattered. His face was a lopsided, bewhiskered raisin topped with a stocking cap. His walk: a hitching gait.

Barbara kept her head down. Avoiding eye contact made it easier to not attract attention. But, damn it, if her brother wasn't heading over to him, hand outstretched, flower at the ready.

"Johnny," she said beneath her voice. "Johnny..."

He turned to her, face like the moon. "Yes?"

"Please," she said softly. "Wait until we're inside."

His reply was joyful. "This cannot wait!"

Barbara hung her head. Kept going. Johnny could catch up with her if he insisted on messing with the homeless guy.

She heard her brother address him: "Can you see the light that is God?"

"Shit no," was his response. "Got any money?"

"Ultimately, we don't need money. We need love." After a slight pause: "A flower for you."

The homeless man raised his crackling voice. "Why the fuck would I need that?" Then it sounded as though he'd slapped Johnny, though hopefully just his hand. As much as Barbara dreaded it, she'd have to go back and extract her brother from the situation.

As she walked the short distance, she got a better look at the homeless guy. The front of his pants was sopping wet, almost down to the knees, and his face was so drawn and tan it resembled a skull. His stench was overpowering, too. Barbara took three steps back, caught a breath then spoke.

"I'm sorry about my brother." She felt awkward, apologizing to a homeless person. Then she felt a little sick as dark, rheumy eyes—tear ducts plugged with yellow matter—met her own. "He's just doing…what he's doing."

"Yeah, and what he's doing is stupid!" The man turned briefly towards her brother. Barbara saw another stain on the seat of his pants. Had to be shit. "Stupid, stupid, stupid!" he shouted at Johnny, then balled up his fist and beat his own head.

She was repulsed. This had to be the weirdest, most vile human being with whom she'd ever conversed. Barbara wished she hadn't thought this, but didn't imagine it was possible for anyone not to think it.

Unperturbed, Johnny held out another flower. Again, the homeless man swatted it away. "I already said I don't want that!"

"I'd love for you to take it, but you needn't accept." Johnny withdrew the flower. "It's a gift one might refuse, but know that I am not sickened by you. You are infused with light, and that light is God!"

Barbara elbowed her brother and whispered, "You're not making this easier." She dug in her purse. "Here," she said to the homeless man. "Have a cigarette."

His eyes widened in shock. "The lady offered me a cigarette!" He flailed his arms and shouted so anyone passing could hear. "Can you believe that? *A cigarette!*"

"Okay, okay! I'll give you two!"

"Two? Who said I wanted one?"

Barbara was astonished. She imagined all homeless men smoked. "I'm sorry," she said, sliding the pack back into her purse. "I—"

"What am I supposed to buy with that…other than *cancer?*"

"I—I really don't know."

"I need money, lady. Not disease and flowers! What the hell is wrong with you people? Are you both crazy?" Then he resumed beating himself on the head.

Barbara decided she'd had enough. She grabbed Johnny

by the crook of his arm and, without a word, made him start walking with her toward the mall.

From behind, she heard shuffling feet.

"Worry not," Johnny said. "Just like us, he is but another of God's creatures."

"I'm not so sure about that."

The homeless man caught up with them. He walked uncomfortably close to Barbara, wet, smelly and grimy clothes brushing against her own. "Just gimme some change, lady. I know yah got it." He pointed at the center of his forehead. "I see it in my mind."

She kept her eyes looking forward. "I already offered you something, and you didn't want it."

"Because what you offered was stupid, stupid, stupid!"

The spots returned. But the situation would resolve itself soon enough. Surely, he wouldn't follow them into the mall.

But when the door closed, the homeless man was there, too.

A security officer, fat and burr-cut, took notice. He cop-walked over to them. "Why did you allow this *individual* to enter with you?" he said, eyes like slits, fists clenched by his hips.

Barbara smelled his breath, noticed his tobacco-stained teeth. "It's not like I asked for it!" she said.

"Don't you realize people are trying to shop without being bothered by some vaga—"

"No, not a vagabond, sir. He is—"

Barbara boxed her brother's shoulder. "Johnny, shut it!" Before addressing the guard, she exhaled rage and inhaled peace. "Instead of going after me, maybe you can just—I don't know—escort the guy from the premises?"

"I should escort *you* from the premises! Inviting him in shows clear disrespect for this mall!" He gestured to the homeless man, now walking in a tight, repetitive circle around them.

"I didn't *invite* him!"

"Then why is he here?"

"Because he followed me!"

Fingers entered belt loops. "So you admit it, then?"

She wanted to say something spicy, but this was a guy with some degree of authority who had the potential to ruin her day. "I didn't admit anything, okay. I just—" Barbara spotted another security officer, waved him over and relaxed a bit. He had to be more sensible.

"This guard," Barbara said, pointing at him once the second arrived. "I don't know what his problem is, but—"

"Lady, I don't know what *your* problem is," barked the new guard.

"Excuse me?"

"Is it just that you attract disgusting people?"

This guard—fat and oily and piggy-faced—was rather disgusting himself. Barbara stumbled on her words. "No, I don't, uh... Just escort him out and we can all be on our merry way!"

The first guard's gaze hardened. His hand hovered over the can of pepper spray attached to his belt. "I don't much like your tone..."

"Okay, okay! I'm sorry! I just think it would be easier if you dealt with that guy, not me."

The guard shook his head. "Making things easy for *you* isn't the point. The point is he came in with you, so he's your responsibility."

"My responsibility!"

"Look, I don't make the laws. I enforce them."

Barbara wanted to retreat into herself, find her happy place. The two security guards on both sides of her, the homeless man circling like a shark as Johnny smiled vacantly—it was all too much. She wished her stress doll were here. She would punch the thing until tatters remained. Instead, she visualized the field again, maintained her cool.

"Shouldn't you be looking for shoplifters?" she said.

That word seemed to trigger something in both guards. The first arched his eyebrows. The second said, "Shoplifters?"

"Yeah, shoplifters. Go find those and—"

"Go find?" He smirked. "I think we found one already."

In her mind, the field began to catch fire. Woodland creatures shrieked. "You just saw me walk in here! How could I have possibly shoplifted yet?"

"Yet? Aha! So you *do* plan to shoplift!"

"What? No! That's not what I said at all! I said—"

The first guard removed a set of handcuffs from his belt. Both advanced.

Anger transitioned to fear. "Look!" Barbara shouted in desperation. "A real shoplifter!" She pointed at no one in particular.

The guards didn't seem convinced, though, at that moment, a scrawny kid in a wife beater walked past, a blaring boom box perched atop his shoulder. "No boom boxes in the mall," the guards said simultaneously. They turned from Barbara, ran to the boy—now wide-eyed—and tackled him to the ground.

Both big men writhed atop his back. His face grew redder; it was hard to tell whether the boy was breathing or not. Still, Barbara took advantage of the opportunity and walked away quickly.

She gave a backwards glance just in time to see the first guard start pepper spraying the kid. The second rose to allow the first to get out his handcuffs, but then did an unexpected thing.

She turned to Johnny. "Did that guard just give the homeless guy a high-five?"

"Huh?" he said.

"Nevermind."

CHAPTER THREE

Barbara really needed that smoothie, and here she was finally in front of the place that sold them.

"I'm going to get my usual," she said to Johnny. "Want anything?"

He smiled. "Only for you to one day see the light that is God."

"I'll take that as a no." She walked towards the counter and the fat, pimple-faced teenaged girl stationed there. "I'll have a cherry vanilla smoothie, please," she said. "Extra large."

The cashier looked at her with a stare so blank Barbara doubted that she'd been heard. Finally, the girl blew a bubble of chewing gum and grabbed a cup, but it wasn't the right size.

"That's a small," Barbara said. "I want extra large."

The girl harrumphed, got a larger cup and turned to a machine to fill it. Spinning back around, she slammed the smoothie on the counter so hard Barbara was surprised the cup didn't split. Then she blew another bubble. "That'll be three dollars."

The smoothie was blue and swimming with green hunks of…something. And it looked sludgy.

"This isn't cherry vanilla," Barbara said. "This is—I don't know what it is."

"Oh, I'm terribly sorry," said the girl in a way that made it seem she wasn't sorry at all. "I'll be right back with your order."

She got another cup, filled it full of stuff from another machine. The moment she turned, Barbara saw the stuff was ice cream.

"No, no, no! Don't even bring that over here!" Barbara

wanted to add more—perhaps she needed to do so—but bit her tongue. She'd just ask politely, yet again, for a goddamn cherry fucking vanilla smoothie.

The girl shrugged at Barbara's request, giggled softly. "It's just one of those days, you know."

Yeah, I know about one of those days. I'm having one right now because of you, but I'm not going to go crazy and I'm not going to scream and I'm not going to dive over the counter and make you eat the shit you're trying to give me, plus my fists. No, I will not do that. You cannot make me.

By the time Barbara finished her mental rant, the girl had placed yet another cup on the counter.

"That's not cherry vanilla, either." The spots made their third appearance of the day. "It's black."

"That's because it's espresso-flavored, available for a limited time only."

She tried to think of the field again. Spots started moving. "If I'd wanted an espresso-flavored smoothie, I would have ordered an espresso-flavored smoothie."

"But it's really good."

Barbara picked up the cup. Smelled it. It reminded her more of sewage than espresso. Spots did the jitterbug. "Just, please, for the love of god, give me a cherry vanilla smoothie." She slid the cup back to the cashier. "It's what I always get when I come here, and I've never had a problem before."

"Well, before you make me go back there again, I'm going to need three dollars."

Before you make me go back there again? How could she say that? The girl had to be an angel or a demon, something sent by God—or whatever—to tempt her this day.

"No, no, no. I'm not paying unless I get what I want, and that's a cherry vanilla smoothie!"

The girl blew a third bubble. "Whatever. Customer's always right." She turned away, but this time didn't go to the machines. She walked into the kitchen area instead.

Minutes passed. Barbara began to wonder what the hell the girl was doing and if she would ever return. When finally she did, she carried a plastic tray piled high with food, at least six wrapped sandwiches, four fries and three large (very large) drinks.

"I'm sorry. I just discovered we're all out of cherry vanilla smoothies, so I brought this stuff instead." She dropped the platter on the counter. "That'll be $34.67."

The flashing spots coalesced, formed a scene. Barbara saw herself grip the girl with hands three times larger than they should be. They kneaded her first, then squeezed, squeezed until ribs crunched and splintered, squeezed until the girl's chest took on an hourglass form and eyes popped out of sockets and into an ice cream tub.

Barbara snuffed the dangerous fantasy, indulged rational thoughts. The girl was a punk ass; she didn't deserve her rage.

Unclenching her teeth, she spoke slowly, calmly. "Okay, I understand you're playing a game. For what reason, I can't say, but I'll just go now; I'll go so I don't have to do what I really, really want and perhaps need to do." Barbara spun around and started walking.

"Thanks!" the girl called. "Have a nice day!"

Barbara gritted her teeth.

CHAPTER FOUR

Barbara turned a corner and saw Johnny address some guy who was talking loudly into a cell phone. He didn't so much as acknowledge him. Her brother then offered a flower to a spindly old lady, complete with a shawl and glasses connected via pearl chain. She whopped him with her purse, and then kept whopping him. Ten times at least. When a teenaged boy with multiple piercings passed, she began to follow and whop him, too.

Maybe if she conversed with Johnny, feigned interest in his religion, it would keep his mind off other people for a while and encourage peace.

"Can we just talk," she said to him, "sister to brother? You can hand out flowers later."

He thought for a few moments, then said, "Okay."

"I'm curious about something."

"What?"

"I just wonder if you ever feel people don't deserve what you offer. Like that old lady. What was her problem?"

He shook his head. "No, my sister, I don't feel that way. Never have and never will."

"Really?"

"They can treat me however they want. It doesn't matter. I've given them the chance to see that we all bathe in God's light, whether we recognize it or not."

Barbara found herself admiring his determination, albeit grudgingly. "What is it, exactly, you want them to see?"

"Again, it's light and love."

"Yeah, but what do you mean by that? Sounds kind of vague to me."

Johnny prattled on about the topic for quite a while,

19

but Barbara didn't hear most of it. She gave the majority of her attention to the gangs of cheerleaders that hung out by the lacy underwear store and in front of the fountain and by the railing of the balcony, enough cheerleaders for six or seven schools. She wondered if this was a multi-county outing of some sort, but then wondered why it consisted exclusively of cheerleaders in uniform.

"And now do you understand?" Johnny said.

Barbara came back to herself. "Uh, I think I do."

"Clearly, it is after we see the light of God that we realize we are not separate from Him. We've just convinced ourselves we are, and that's the source of all the Earth's problems."

"That sort of makes sense."

"It makes all the sense in the world."

Just ahead of them, an old woman was leaving the drug store. A stern young woman in a blue blazer slammed the door in her face as she exited. The older woman did not fall, but made a shocked then angry face at the younger woman through the glass.

Wow, Barbara thought. *What an asshole.*

She heard something rattle. Looking down, she watched Johnny pull a tambourine from a deep pocket in his robe.

Shit. She hadn't realized he carried one of those. Had she known, it might have been a deal-breaker. People outside the shops leered at them. Barbara thought of the security guards again; she didn't want to risk their continued attention. "No, Johnny," she said. "Now's not the time to do this."

His smiled widened. He beat the tambourine, harder and harder against his hip.

"Come on, we just got here. Can't we look around a bit first?"

"I can't turn off Bliss, my sister. To do so would be to insult the Light, and I've vowed never to do that again."

"Okay, Johnny. That's good. You should…shine God's Light. Yes."

His gaze grew distant. His grip on the instrument slackened, and he began to chant. "Kunamunahanatantumakiyan…"

She waited until he stopped. "Is that even a human language?"

He started again, shaking the tambourine this time. "Kemanatahanapatamanaha…"

Barbara really wished she had that smoothie now.

CHAPTER FIVE

As time passed, Barbara realized she'd definitely picked the wrong day to go to the mall. She watched a middle-aged man being hassled by yet another group of cheerleaders. They were stubborn—chattering all around, acting as though they were interested in him when clearly it was a cruel game. They turned once he broke free from their orbital, surging forward until they located another homely male at the corner of the bookstore.

The first man continued walking. Sweaty now. He kept going until a gang of toughs dressed like it was *West Side Story* met him by the computer store and tossed sticky-looking trash at him from a bin. Another security guard stood nearby. He had to see what was going on, but did nothing. A fellow shopper tried to help, and was pelted, too.

Barbara turned from the display just as Johnny offered a flower to yet another person.

"A flower? Go fuck yourself!" said the kid. He couldn't have been older than five.

"Maybe you should cut the flower stuff for now," Barbara suggested. Logically, there wouldn't be so many assholes at the mall next week, or even tomorrow.

"No," he replied. "These people need desperately to experience the eternal love that is God. All this is happening for a reason."

Yeah, she thought, *to annoy me.*

Suddenly, a voice behind her: "You've got a sexy ass." She turned, though the slick, oily-looking man wasn't talking to her, but a pretty young blonde who seemed nothing if not offended.

"Wanna go out to my van and watch some videos?" he continued.

Did she just hear that? No, she didn't. Barbara kept walking.

Someone came up behind her. She jumped. It was a balding man in a white suit, carrying a golden platter on which turd-shaped chocolates had been arranged. "Care for a sample?" he asked.

Barbara winced. "No, thank you."

"How about now?"

"I said no."

He moved the platter behind his back. It reemerged covered in bite-sized chicken sandwiches. She had no idea how he managed that.

"These more to your liking?"

Johnny held out a flower and Barbara scowled at him. "Really, cut the flower shit!"

The man kept following. "You didn't answer me. Are they to your liking? If not, I can offer something else."

Barbara scrunched her lips, said nothing.

"Come on, you can tell me."

This couldn't be happening. Not a bit of it seemed real.

"I assure you, they're the best money can—"

Someone gripped his shoulder from behind. Barbara turned and saw it was a taller, brown-haired (and rather handsome) man. "Can't you see you're bothering this lady?" he said. "Scram!" He addressed Barbara. "It's sad, but people have no taste nowadays."

"Thanks so much. I've never known—"

From behind his back, he removed a platter, brimming with sandwiches. "My samples are far superior to his. That place uses compressed, liquefied chicken. Disgusting, right? Well, *The Chicken Shack* uses only fresh and bounteous breasts!"

"Oh my God!"

A woman appeared on her other side. "Perfume?" She began to spray hideous-smelling toilet water all over Barbara's blouse.

23

Then another person jumped in front of her. "Candied peanuts?" he said.

And other: "Summer sausage?"

And another: "Carmel popcorn?" And another: "Pitted prunes?" And another: "Yak butter?"

Yak butter?

The cavalcade was endless. Even Johnny seemed overwhelmed. Barbara saw an opening—just a small strand of light—betwixt the wall of people. She grabbed Johnny by the arm, crashed through the wall and ran with him to the closest door.

A few seconds passed before she realized she'd found her way into the men's bathroom. One of the stalls was occupied. A toilet flushed. The stall door opened, a man exited, and dear sweet lord if he wasn't another Hare Krishna, only clad in a pink robe instead of white, the front of which was covered by a huge, red letter S.

"Hey, Asshole!" said the man to Johnny, convivially.

"Excuse me?" Johnny said.

"Wait, you're not..." He smirked. "Oh..."

Johnny walked up to the man. "I am so glad to see a fellow Hare Krishna here today! Such great encouragement!" He regarded the man's robe. "But tell me, what does the big S mean?"

The man tapped his chest. "It means I'm a Super-Hare Krishna."

Johnny knitted his brows. "Super-Hare Krishna?"

"Indeed. We Super-Hare Krishnas have the ability to reflect more God Light than the average Hare Krishna, hence we are Super."

For the first time since his conversion, Barbara saw Johnny's ever-placid face start to look pissed. "Are you sure you're a Hare Krishna? Have you ever been to a Hare Krishna service?"

"No, I have not attended even a single service. I do not need to; I am beyond such artifacts."

"And have you spoken with another Hare Krishna prior to speaking with me?"

"Myself, before I became a Super-Hare Krishna."

Johnny almost shouted. "I meant someone apart from yourself!"

"No one is apart from myself, not when looked at in the True Light."

His fists clenched. "What do you know of the True Light?"

"More than you, that's for sure. I even sew my own clothes." The Super-Hare Krishna stared Johnny down. "Can you say the same?"

"No, but I don't see how—"

"Sewing my own clothes makes me an even deeper Super-Hare Krishna, because I have the devotion to wear only the things I create. Of course, I don't expect someone like yourself to understand."

A part of Barbara wanted to butt in, perhaps deck the Super-Hare Krishna for being such an ass, but maybe it would take this for her brother to understand his new religion wasn't perfect, and he'd return to being Regular Johnny again.

"I beg to differ," her brother continued. "All of humanity reflects the same amount of light, and that light is infinite. You can call yourself *Super*, but know, deep down, that we are all the same."

The Super-Hare Krishna flapped his hands in mimicry of a mouth. "Blah, blah, blah... When you talk that's all I hear."

Barbara noted Johnny's reddening forehead. "I thought I'd found a brother, but I was wrong. You are full of darkness." He extended his hand. "Here, I think you really need this flower."

"No, I don't want your stupid little flower." With a sudden sneer; he shouted, "I'd rather you shove it so far up your ass that petals shoot from your mouth!" He grabbed the front of Johnny's robe, pulled it up and wrapped it over Johnny's head and around his neck.

"Nice panties," sneered the Super-Hare Krishna. "Your mother buy them for you?" Then he pushed Johnny into the toilet he'd just used.

Their conversation had been almost amusing for a while, but it had gone too far. It hurt, seeing her brother debased, so she would hurt this guy in return, hurt him physically.

Barbara stalked up to the man, fists at the ready. "Just what do you think—"

"Stay back, lady! This is between me and the dumb-ass."

"No, I will not! And that dumb-ass is my—"

At that moment, an angry voice from the toilet: "Barbara, no! This is my battle!"

She turned. Johnny had risen. He lowered his robe and wiped his face. There was rage in his eyes that Barbara hadn't expected to see.

"Ha, ha," said the Super-Hare Krishna. "You think you can better me, panty-man? Fat chance."

"I wear briefs, okay! Not panties!"

"Whatever, Panty Krishna."

Johnny groaned. Lowering his head like a bull, he ran until it impacted against the stomach of the Super-Hare Krishna. Barbara felt proud; her brother was finally asserting himself.

"Look here, asshole!" Johnny said as the other man winced and clutched his gut. "You're going to take these motherfucking flowers and like them!" He bashed the entire bouquet over the man's head and then thrust the ruined flowers into his arms. "There you go, you prick!"

The man glanced up, smiled. Barbara found that to be an odd reaction.

Obviously, her brother did, too. He stepped back, confusion spreading across his face. That confused look shifted quickly to one of unease, then of pain. He clutched his head and squinted. His cheeks reddened. He exhaled in heavy, irregular bursts.

"Johnny? What's wrong?"

"I—I don't… Oh god, it hurts!"

The Super-Hare Krishna kept smiling from the floor as Barbara reached out to her brother and took him in her arms. He flailed, so she clutched him tighter. It was the only thing she knew to do.

Johnny's spasms intensified. His contours began to feel different, unfamiliar. His robe turned half brown/half white, split in the center, became less flowing and more akin to a pair of pants and a t-shirt. No, not *more like*.

Was.

"Johnny?" She pulled away, looked at him. The face that met hers was not her brother's countenance, but a younger, wider, pug-nosed face, ruddy and apparently drunk, like a particularly surly British soccer fan. He had hair now, too: short, curly, and brown. His t-shirt said *Property of Shitwanshire Rugby League.*

The Super-Hare Krishna stood, wrapped his arms around her ex-brother's shoulder. "Now you are *my* brother!" he told him.

Barbara froze into place, staring at the two strangers before her, unaware she wasn't breathing.

"What yah lookin' at, yah cunt?" her non-brother, now thickly accented, spat. Then he took a big gulp of lager from a pint glass he couldn't possibly have.

She was screaming before she was aware of it. Paralysis broke, and Barbara took off running.

CHAPTER SIX

Her scream was a siren-call. Faces turned to her as she fled the bathroom, hundreds if not thousands of them. Almost everyone in the mall, coming toward her, arms outstretched, eyes hungry. Mouths, too. A few shoppers looked confused, or even terrified, just like Barbara. But she didn't have time to help them. She had to keep running.

Behind her, a litany of voices:

"You'll buy this dress! It'll look great on your fat ass!"

"Free tickets! Free tickets even if you don't want 'em!"

"Can I interest you in a timeshare?"

Barbara sprinted through a gauntlet of security personnel amassed near the exit. Dodging clouds of pepper spray, she saw the two guards she'd dealt with earlier. They had a pregnant woman in a headlock. A young man screamed curses at them; his t-shirt became a sweater, his pants a skirt. Barbara didn't consider this. She barreled out the door from which she'd entered, ran across the expanse of the parking lot, jumped into her car and started it up.

People pressed themselves against the windshield, faces leering, fists pounding.

"50 percent off!" a man clutching a purple dress screamed. "*50 percent off!*" Another tried to force a box full of chicken nuggets on her by placing it under the left windshield wiper. A note was attached to it: YOU WILL EAT THESE!

Barbara tore across the parking lot, traveled over the median and shot out onto the street. With her free hand, she reached into her purse for the cell phone. She had to call her mother and tell her not to go to the mall. She punched buttons, but the phone was a lifeless hunk of

28

plastic in her hand. "Fuck!"

If the phone wouldn't work, then she had to go to her mother's place. Barbara made an illegal U-turn.

CHAPTER SEVEN

Soon, a bunch of laborers plastering up a billboard caught her eye. Just before she passed, Barbara realized one of them was mooning the cars below as he worked.

Seconds later, she stopped at a red light. At least six drivers behind her started blowing their horns.

"The light's red!" Barbara shouted out the window.

"We fucking know!" someone shouted back.

"Then what's the problem?"

"We wanna go, but you're standing in our way!"

"What?!"

"Go, Lady! Just go! Go! Go!"

To hell with it. She floored the gas pedal. The other drivers floored their pedals, too.

She passed a cop car, but it didn't do anything. The cop had been one of those behind her in line, beeping.

CHAPTER EIGHT

On the next street over, a car traveled alongside Barbara's, neck and neck. She turned and looked at the driver: a greasy guy with long hair, bedecked in a ratty old band shirt. He made his fingers into a devil's sign, lolled his tongue out at her and bopped his head.

"Your car sucks donkey!" he shouted. "I challenge you to a race!"

The guy drove a peeling white station wagon from the early 80s. Barbara pressed down the accelerator, passed him in a blur, then passed another cop car, unmanned and on the side of the road, flashing speeds via a jutting LCD sign.

86 miles per hour, it said for her.

Soon, she spotted a roving, loosely knit assembly of middle-aged businessmen, busily knocking down and reversing street signs, or painting over them with obscenities or crudely rendered genitalia. Immediately afterwards, she saw three kids—one boy and two girls—holding up an ice cream man in his truck.

Those have to be toy guns. Those have to be toy guns, she thought, a mantra of her own.

CHAPTER NINE

Barbara reached her mother's driveway within eight minutes of leaving the mall. Ordinarily, it would have taken twenty.

The first thing she noticed: workers piling out her mother's front door. Some carried tables, others chairs and rugs. Everything, it seemed, was en route to one of four big white vans parked across the street.

Barbara bounded from her car. Brushing past workers, she raced up porch steps to the door. Inside, there were more of them, dozens of big, smelly guys, moving her mother's delicate things, grinding tables into door facings and knocking vases and Hummel figurines to the floor.

A man stood in the center of the room, clipboard in hand. Late middle-aged, he was squat and balding and dressed differently from the rest in a button-up shirt and slacks.

"Who are you?" Barbara asked. "What are you doing here?"

"I'm the landlord," he replied.

Landlord? She was almost sure her mother had bought the place.

He tapped a pen on his clipboard. "And I'm here because Mrs. Adams is three months behind on her rent, so we're taking all this shit until she coughs it up!"

"What?" A worker bumped into Barbara. She scowled at him and turned back to the landlord. "You can't do this!"

"Rest assured, I can."

The world started to swim. "Where is she? Where's my mother?"

"Last I saw that loud old biddy, she was upstairs."

Her mother wasn't loud; she was reserved, quiet, and didn't bother anyone. But Barbara let the insult wash over and past her. She just had to find her mother, set things straight. Afterwards, she could pound the man until he was a jellied lump on the floor.

Barbara hastened to the staircase. A sofa filled up the bottom quarter. She shouted at the closest worker. "Move this sofa!"

"We'll move it when we're ready to move it," he said.

"Yeah, you're not our boss," another added, then dumped her mother's books from a shelf.

To hell with them. Barbara clamored across the sofa, digging into the pillows for purchase. She clawed up to the armrest and jumped onto a step. Upstairs, she darted into each room she passed, called her mother's name, but was answered with silence.

She came to the master bedroom last. As before, the space was utterly vacant. The bed seemed like a catalogue prop, the rocking chair like a forgotten antique. It felt as though her mother's presence had been drawn completely from the house. But car keys were on the dresser; her purse was where she always kept it. Barbara looked into the small adjoining bathroom. It was empty, too.

She ran back down the stairs, over the sofa and to the landlord.

"My mother's not up there!" Barbara fought the urge to grab the collar of the man's shirt and bring him down. "Where is she?"

"Look, lady. I already—"

"Tell me!"

He just shrugged, lit a foul smelling cigar.

Suddenly, the unthinkable occurred to her. If her brother had changed, then maybe her mom had changed, too. She thought for a few seconds, bit her lip and then gave voice to madness. "Are you…my mother?"

"Do I look like I have a vagina?" He blew a huge gray

plume into her face.

Barbara stepped back. The man probably wasn't her mother. He was probably the one who'd changed her. She looked around. Her mom, she figured, had to be one of the workers.

She approached a hulking Hispanic man in a blue muscle shirt, looked into his eyes. "Are you my mother?"

"*Que?*"

"If you're in there, I need for you to hear this!"

"*Que?*" he reiterated.

"I love you, Mom! I love you so much!"

The man brushed past her, grabbed an end table and shook things from it violently. Barbara turned to the next closest worker, posed the same question.

He clenched his jaw. "Could somebody move this crazy bitch so I can do my job?"

She spun from him, queried six others. Most were too busy disposing of her mother's things to make eye contact. One laughed.

"Please, Mom!" she roared to the room in general. "Just say *something!*"

Barbara heard only the sound of mulling workers, of things beating against other things, of glass breaking and wood splintering. She became aware of her heartbeat then; she'd never felt it pound so hard. Farther up, her brain pulsed, seemed hot. She needed air, stability, to be anywhere but where she was. Screaming, she ran from the house.

Outside, a guy stood by her car, messing with its radio antennae and kicking its body with one foot and then the other.

The world in front of her went red. Barbara's system shifted to rage-induced autopilot, and she was moving towards him before she realized it. His acts were relatively minor, but he'd made himself available at the right time to become a living stress doll.

The man noted her approach. He offered up a shit-eating grin; a car sped out from an adjacent side street and smashed his body against her mother's favorite tree.

She wasn't sure what had just happened; a movie must be playing in her head. But no, there was the car, the front crumpled and reeking of spilled fluids, and the man—oh god, he must be dead, his body cut in half at the waist and leaking just like the car. She smelled fecal matter over gasoline and wanted to vomit.

Barbara spun. She saw workers moving things out of her mother's place as though nothing was wrong.

"Somebody, call 911!" she shouted.

One gave her the middle finger with a free hand. (*Mother?*) The rest ignored her.

She turned back around. The driver stared at her through spider web cracks in safety glass, his mouth a red gash, studded with broken teeth.

"Are you okay?" she shouted, and felt stupid for asking.

He smiled. "I'm very much okay." When he stepped out of his car, the hole in his stomach gushed blood, yawned wide. "And sorry for the theatrics," he continued, "but they got your attention, right?"

Barbara watched the man's intestines start to spill out. The other man, the one splattered against the tree, waved. "Jesus loves you!" he gurgled.

The driver then gestured to the ruined car, the other ruined man. "What happened to us could easily happen to you...and since you're not like us, you'd go somewhere." He gave a too-wide smile. "Tell me, would that place be Hell?"

Barbara babbled, and the man advanced, his guts continuing to unwind. "Yeah, I think it would be," he said. "You wear too much makeup and dress like a slut."

"This is just my—I didn't even—I—"

He spoke over her. "Maybe you worship that fat guy. Or one of those fifty-armed, elephant-headed girls. Or *the void*, whatever that may be. But let me tell you, those gods are stupid and lame, and people who worship them are no better. Only Jesus saves."

The guy had to be dead. Dead and gone. Both of them, in fact. But there they were, moving, talking, trying to help her find the Lord.

His smile faltered a bit. "You're not an atheist are you? You're beginning to sound like one."

"Please— No—"

"Atheists are another matter entirely." He paused a beat. "We hate atheists and have a very special way of dealing with them."

"Yeah!" screamed the other man. "We make them wear the headgear!" Then he coughed up blood.

The approaching Christian removed a collapsible helmet from his pocket. It brimmed with coiled wires and knobs. Tiny red lights flashed on and off. "This'll *make* you believe," he said.

The Christian lunged at her. Barbara moved quickly to his left and slid in the pool of his spilled guts.

"Heathen!" he screamed. "Heretic!"

Barbara regained her balance and took off running. Suddenly, she felt separate from her body. She observed it from on high, her brain swimming in the ether. It was time to get herself back in the car. It was just a matter of feet away. Not far at all. She'd take those steps and go. Go home. Go quickly. Take a bath and wash off the madness. Slide into bed and sleep away the horror.

Yes.

CHAPTER TEN

Barbara was driving without memory of having gotten into the car. Driving. Driving. Driving.

Was her mother dead? Had that man killed her…or… No, she didn't even want to think that thought. She tried to dial 9-11, but her fingers didn't work.

"I'm drunker than shit, lady!" sloshed the driver across from her.

Ignore him. Ignore him. Not real. Not real.

Cars around her increased their speed. She had to keep going. Past 120 mph. Past 130, 280 and 360. Go with the flow. Do it or be killed.

Did that van just explode?

Don't know. Don't know. Don't know.

And were people changing into other people, en masse, while screaming on the sidewalk or in the middle of the road?

Can't think about that now. Can't think about that now.

Her tires bumped over a corpse. Or she thought it was a corpse. It was man-shaped, crisp and blackened. Probably just an old garbage bag, though. Had to be.

The drunk voice again: "Wanna bottle, baby?"

Something smashed against the partially open window. Amber liquid splattered her. She didn't turn around, not even as the drunk driver swerved into her lane.

There was the sound of shrieking metal. Barbara's car went over the median, clear across the other side of the street past a fire hydrant and between two tall shrubs. She saw this. Was powerless to stop it, or even to think all that hard about current events. Things were just happening. Things always happened.

The car smashed against something tall. A tree, maybe?

37

An oak tree. A maple tree. A hanging tree. Who knew? Barbara knew nothing. She'd hit her head on the steering wheel when the hood buckled and blacked out.

CHAPTER ELEVEN

The world was a blur. Barbara didn't recognize herself as existing in it.

Suddenly, a face: "Are you awake?"

Another face: "Lady, are you awake?"

She became aware of herself. Things came slowly into focus. Seven, maybe eight, men hovered over her. They wore concerned expressions on young and somewhat stupid-looking faces. Some were slightly overweight. All wore cargo shorts, and a few were shirtless, but those who sported them had t-shirts branded with the initials of a college: AHU.

Barbara realized she was seeing them from the wrong angle, provided she was still in the driver's seat. She felt something slick beneath her. Damp grass. Someone must have dragged her out of the car. Was it on fire? At least she still had her purse. She couldn't see it, but felt it resting against her stomach.

She lifted a hand to her forehead. "I'm fine. I'm okay," she said. "I think—I think I must have had a wreck."

"Are you sure you're okay?" said one voice.

"Are you *really* sure?" echoed another.

"Yes, I'm sure. I just want to stand."

"That's good. That's really good. But you can't stand. Not yet."

"What? Why not?"

A pudgy face smiled. "First, you've got to agree to a date, hot stuff."

"Date me, too!" said the skinniest one.

"And me!" said one in sunglasses and a backwards baseball cap.

"Then you gotta fuck us! Woohoo!" slurred a new voice.

Visibly drunk, its owner stumbled in from behind the others, belched, and ran stubby hands through Barbara's hair.

She recoiled, tried to get up, but the frat boys were packed in too tightly around her.

"You a lesbian?" The drunk guy grabbed his crotch, hiked up his junk. "Only a lesbian wouldn't want what I've got."

Another: "Cool it down, Larry. Maybe she's still a virgin."

Larry unbuttoned his shorts, revealing the top of his fire engine red underwear. "How about a quick blowjob, then. It's not *real* sex."

"You can still be a virgin and do it," the skinny one agreed.

"You wouldn't even have to swallow," added a shirtless one.

"The hell she wouldn't!" Larry dropped his shorts, but immediately tripped on them. He stumbled backwards into the skinniest one, creating a gap. Barbara pulled herself from the ground and pushed herself through it.

The frat boys gave chase, the drunk one still in his jockeys. "Don't mind Larry!" the skinniest shouted. "We'll treat you like a princess!"

Barbara turned. Behind them, she noticed her car, wrapped around a tree below a high ledge. It looked totaled. No matter. She kept running. Though the world swayed, she felt she could outpace her pursuers.

Suddenly, a group consisting of five teenaged girls wearing tight spandex pants and gauzy blouses poured out from between two bushes. All had pink, puffy hair.

"Look at her!" said one girl, pointing, giggling. "What a train wreck!"

"Remind me not to go to her stylist," said another. Then all ran towards her.

Shit! Where are these assholes coming from?

The quickest girl reached her mark. "And she's got a *huge* nose!" the teen shouted. Her breath—rank, but with a hint of mint-flavored freshener—washed over Barbara.

"And terrible skin," said the first. "Have you ever seen so many blemishes?"

"It's like blackhead city," a third agreed.

A fourth grabbed her blouse, commented on its shoddy workmanship. Barbara was pulled back just long enough for the frat boys to catch up.

"We'll get you drunk! We'll get you drunk!" the guys exclaimed, reforming the circle with the girls who continued to insult her fashion sense.

Contradictory messages sent Barbara reeling. Then came the groping hands. She gasped for air, felt on the verge of suffocation. "Stop touching me!" she choked. "Stop!" Closing her eyes, she flailed her arms and legs until she'd freed herself.

There was a home in the near distance—a white, two-story farmhouse, backed and flanked by dense woods. Barbara turned her trajectory towards it. Looked old, imposing, like the sort of thing an early landowner might have built for his family, and she wasn't sure why she was thinking such thoughts when a bunch of crazy people hooted and hollered just behind her.

She reached the porch—sagging and rickety—and crossed its seemingly too-long expanse. She slammed her fists against a door at least twelve feet tall. "Let me in!" she screamed. "Please!"

Not far behind her: "Don't worry! We won't gang bang you!" Slightly farther back: "I wouldn't be caught dead in those shoes!"

Her fists started to ache. "I need help!"

The steps creaked, a host of feet treading them. Fuck it. She tried the knob. It moved, and she felt a rush that almost left her giddy.

Inside, she slammed the door then turned the lock below its knob. There was a deadbolt above it, but the sort that could only be operated with a key. A table was to the left of the door. On it: a ring with two keys attached. The first didn't work, but the second fastened the deadbolt. She put the key in her blouse pocket, ran into the kitchen where most likely there was another door.

It was unlocked, too. Just as she reached for the knob, it turned. A soft, well-manicured hand slipped in, gripped the facing. Barbara pushed it back and kicked the door shut. Another deadbolt key was on the counter. She put it to quick use.

"You're even uglier now!" shouted the voice on the other side.

Barbara didn't reply. She ran from the kitchen and went around the first floor of the house, looking for other doors but finding none. Still, she continued her search, circling rooms repeatedly. Maybe there was another door, a secret and hidden one. Maybe she wasn't looking hard enough.

The house's interior was uninviting, vast and old looking, full of weird knickknacks and interior wind chimes. Serial-killer rustic. One of the rooms had at least thirty animal heads mounted on the wall. Maws were wide, teeth were bared and glass eyes leered. Another room had a porcelain music box, sculpted to look like a ballerina. Barbara thought about that music box as she searched for unlocked doors. She wondered what melody it might make even as individual rooms started to seem like parts of a funhouse maze and things before her eyes became more like streaks than discernable objects. She had no idea why the music box entranced her so.

Exhausted, she collapsed against a wall and slid down it. She thought she might investigate upstairs later. Maybe there'd be a gun in a closet or dresser somewhere. First, however, she needed to rest, that and have a cigarette. She could die with a cigarette.

She fished the pack from her purse, shook it. Four smokes left.

Damn.

At the very least, Barbara was thankful for the homeless man's earlier refusal. She lit the cigarette. Maybe the people who owned the place were upstairs and would be pissed to find a strange woman in their house, clogging it with smoke. Oh well. They'd just have to deal with it.

She inhaled the first drag and held it like marijuana. This would be no five-minute smoke; she would take it slow, revel in nicotine.

Fifteen minutes later, after the cigarette had been reduced to filter, Barbara peeked out a window. The people were still there, some wandering aimlessly, others staring at the door or sitting on grass and pulling at the strands as though bored. One, however—a new arrival—talked on a cell phone and stared at her as she watched.

Barbara replaced the curtain quickly. Then it dawned on her. If his cell phone worked, hers should, too. She hadn't gotten along well with her sister, not at all. Now, she felt the need to call her, make things right, though not before first trying 911.

The phone remained dead. Barbara wanted to crush the thing in her palm. Instead, she looked out the window, a bit more discretely this time. The man still chattered away.

CHAPTER TWELVE

In a den adjoining the living room, Barbara found an old TV. A darkly stained grandfather clock loomed over it— gothic-looking ornamentation on the hood and bonnet. Barbara didn't like standing in its shadow.

She bent down, turned the TV on and flicked the knob that changed the channels, encountering bands of static until she reached channel 31.

The static was still there, but, if she squinted, Barbara could barely discern a male form, seated at what appeared to be a desk. His voice seemed covered by the ocean, then by the wind. Still, she was able to glean fragments of what he said:

"Because of the threat...untold number...citizens... and due to...now developing...a sudden explosive epidemic of...in cities and suburbs across...eyewitnesses describe them as rude or... and aggressive...weird...quite possibly insane..."

"Come on!" Barbara hit the top of the TV. "Work!" But the picture grew snowier, the audio less discernable.

"...law...reaction...mayhem...inside...locked doors...presidential...at 8...and—"

Static overtook the channel completely. Still, she watched it for five more minutes, hoping the sound might at least return. It never did.

The time had come, Barbara figured, to try the rooms upstairs.

Apprehensively, she approached a tall, dark staircase. The steps and railing-top had been worn slick from years of foot and hand traffic.

"Hello!" she called out. "Anyone up there?"

There was only silence.

Barbara ascended the stairs. They creaked. Boards were loose; a few seemed ready to break. She was glad once she reached the top, but less glad it was so dark and there didn't appear to be a light switch.

Something by her feet—something small and white—caught her eye. She bent down. It was a piece of paper. On it, an all-caps note:

THERE SHOULD BE A BLOODY SKELETON HERE. SORRY.

It implied the house had been recently occupied, or maybe that it had been used as a haunted house last Halloween. It was the one logical reason for bloody skeleton-placement Barbara could conceive.

She stepped over the paper, entered the hallway. It twisted and folded weirdly. She turned one corner and then another, then three more, sometimes within inches of the last bend. Soon, she traveled in a spiral, the path eating its own tail.

There seemed to be no doors or windows, and while there was just enough light to see a foot or two in front of and behind her, its source remained elusive.

Still, Barbara kept going, if only to convince herself of her sanity. Rooms had to be up here, somewhere, but all she passed were identical white walls, void of ornamentation.

A hundred more twists and turns of darkness. Finally, she saw the first hint of difference: a square of light in the distance.

She took off running. The path had finally evened out, but the square never increased in size, not even as she passed through it and spilled out into the kitchen.

Barbara stumbled around a bit, felt drunk. It was best, she imagined, not to think too hard about how she'd gotten there from the hall upstairs.

CHAPTER THIRTEEN

In the living room, a phone started ringing.

Did she want to answer it? Not really, but what if somebody sane was on the other end, somebody who'd help her, or knew somebody who could? Then again, the caller was probably acquainted with the people who owned the house, and he or she would no doubt wonder why someone named Barbara had answered the call.

Conflicted, she left the kitchen and just stared at the phone for a matter of seconds. Then she reached out, hand almost touching the receiver. She couldn't convince herself to pick it up before the ringing stopped.

Barbara wondered whether hesitation had been a good or bad thing. She guessed she'd never know.

The phone rang again.

She picked up the receiver. "H-hello…" she said.

"Hi!" replied the cheery, fast-talking male voice. "How are you today?"

"F-fine," Barbara replied, almost instinctually, and then realized what she had said.

"Wonderful," he continued before she could correct the mistake. "Now, I'm going to ask you a few short survey questions. Please answer them to the best—"

Barbara collected herself. "No, wait! I'm not fine at all! I'm in lots of trouble, and I need you to call the police for me!"

Silence, followed by an exasperated sigh. "Can't you call them yourself?"

"My phone's messed up!"

"Maybe you should buy a new one."

She flailed her free arm. "I don't have time to do that! Please, just—"

46

The voice adopted a patronizing lilt. "Listen, miss. A lot is riding on this survey. I'm sure it's more important than whatever little thing troubles you."

Barbara wrapped her hand tighter around the receiver, pretending it was this guy's neck. Still, she spoke coherently: "No, you listen. There's a bunch of crazy shit happening. I don't know what to do, and I can't get a hold of anyone unless you help me. So please—*please*—call the police and tell them—"

"Sorry, but it really isn't my concern. I'm not paid to help you; I'm paid to collect your information."

"You don't understand!"

Following a slight pause: "I understand you're going to take my survey."

"No! You must—"

"You on the rag or something?" He huffed. "Whatever. I don't give a fuck. First question: Are you now or have you ever—"

Barbara slammed down the receiver; the phone rang a third time.

"What!" she shouted into it.

A different voice, this time female: "Hello, there. I'm taking donations for the International Raped Burned and Blind Orphans Fund, or RBBOF for short. Might you be interested in making a large charitable donation?"

"No!"

"All I need are your credit card and social security numbers, complete bank account information, mother's maiden name and—"

Barbara didn't bother to hang up. She yanked the cord that connected the phone out of the wall, grabbed the thing and lifted it above her head. She smashed it against the floor until pieces of black plastic mingled on the floor with the phone's shattered guts.

At that moment, her stomach started to churn. She felt sick, having realized she'd destroyed her only real

47

connection to the outside world. If the phone received calls, then it could make them, and she could have dialed her mother, her sister, 911...

Barbara wanted to smack herself. There was no one else to smack. The place wasn't equipped with its own stress doll, she was sure.

Maybe I can make one. A big bag of flour, some broken broomsticks for arms and—

The sound of a car engine dashed her thoughts. When it stopped, she heard a door slam. A feminine voice screamed, "Look at his horrible, crinkly hair!"

Barbara ran to the closest window, but the view it offered was slightly to the left of the action. A protruding bay further obscured things.

Seconds later: a pounding at the door. She cursed the lack of a peephole. Then she heard another voice, deep and masculine yet colored by fear. "Is anyone in there?"

"Hello?" Barbara said through the door.

"Oh thank god! Let me in!"

She reached in her pocket for the key and felt nothing but lint.

Continued pounding. "I can't take much more of this!" Suddenly, a cry of desperation: "Stop touching me, please!"

She checked her pants pockets, though she was sure she hadn't put the key there. The only thing she found: an old bubblegum wrapper.

"Jesus, lady! I'd appreciate it if you'd hurry the fuck up!"

"Shit! I think—I think the key must have fallen out of my pocket!"

"God, they're all over my jock!"

Barbara couldn't bear the man's voice. She had to find that key, and just hoped it hadn't dropped somewhere upstairs. She said, "I'll be back in a second!" then realized how lame that sounded. Getting down on her hands and knees, she looked left and right, scurried across the living room floor and into the kitchen.

From there, she heard a second new voice, louder than the others. It hitched and stuttered behind the door, like the speaker suffered from Tourettes.

"You…You're a Neg—a Negroid. Chicken-brained Negroid. Pigeon-toed N-Negroid. Negroid, Negroid, N-Negroid."

"Okay! You're right!" said the poor man. "I admit it! I'm a Negroid!"

"That's—that's right you are! Negroid, Negroid, N-Negroid!"

"I said it's true! *All true!*" Then a shout intended for Barbara: "I'm going to have to punch a hole in someone if you don't hurry!"

"I'm trying, okay!" she screamed over her shoulder.

"Come—" A choir of insults subsumed his words just as Barbara caught a glimpse of gold below the kitchen door.

"I found it!" she said, more to herself than the stranger, and sprinted back into the living room, key in hand. The front door rattled in its frame. Barbara hoped it was because the man was knocking so hard, not because he was being knocked so hard against it.

"I'm here!" she shouted. "I've got the key!"

"Great! Now let me in!"

She rammed the key into the deadbolt, turned it, unfastened the second lock and opened the door. A strapping black man in khaki slacks and white button-up shirt clawed his way inside. Arms followed him, flopping around the facing, hands grasping at air or clutching at trim. Barbara pushed back the weaker ones. The man put his weight against the door. "I'm sorry you can't come in," he said. "So sorry."

Barbara was confused.

Eventually, the stubborn arms withdrew and the door slammed shut. As soon as the locks were engaged, the man scurried about the room, diving onto coffee tables, end tables and any other sort of table he could find, smashing them, taking out legs and stealing their tops. Then he turned against the bookshelves, a whirlwind of manic activity.

"What are you doing?" Barbara asked.

"I'll answer later!" he shouted back. "Got to find more wood! Look for wood!"

Barbara just stood there, wondering, perhaps, if she hadn't let in one of the crazy people.

"Are you looking?"

"Yes, yes! I'm looking!"

"Try the kitchen! I'll try the basement!"

Barbara obeyed on reflex. The kitchen table, she imagined, was the largest hunk of unattached wood in the room, but she had no idea what to do with it. Smash it like the man had smashed the other pieces? But to what end?

The man came up behind her, sheets upon sheets of plywood cradled in his left arm, assorted tools in his right, two-by-fours jutting over both shoulders. Barbara jumped on sight. How had he gotten up from the basement so quickly?

"Don't just look at it!" he snarled. "Rip that fucker apart!"

She turned the table over on its side, kicked at thick oak legs until they fell away. The top was too heavy to carry alone, so she picked up a wooden cutting board and brought it to the living room to have something to show.

There, Barbara stared in amazement at the pile the man had collected. She wondered how it was possible for one house to offer up such a bounty in so short a time. Maybe a woodshop or storeroom was in the basement. Or a frickin' wholesaler.

The man appeared to hump a piano. He glared at her cutting board. "Is that all you've got?"

"I took the legs off the kitchen table, too!"

His face relaxed. "Good, but don't drag the table here. We'll need it in the kitchen when we board up that door."

"We're boarding up doors?"

"Hell yeah!" He detached the piano top, threw it in the growing pile. "Windows, too!"

It seemed a bit like overkill to her. Doors were sturdy and she imagined that, if it were their aim, the crazies would have already gone for the windows. "There really aren't that many—"

"No, you don't understand! They're biding their time. They've got us trapped, and they know it. There'll be more soon, lady. I guarantee that. And when they come, we don't want to be just standing around. We've got to board this place up!"

"We ran here. Can't we just run somewhere else if we have to?"

"Not if there's a wall of them!"

"So let's leave before the wall gets here!"

"And where exactly would we go?"

Barbara shrugged. "To our families, I guess. To the police. Somewhere safe."

"Somewhere safe?" He flung up his hands. "*Somewhere safe* doesn't exist anymore! That's not the same world out there. It's changed and it's going to keep changing until it's nothing at all like you and I know!"

"But—"

"No! Listen to me! Some of these assholes aren't just total dicks. They're rampaging fucking maniacs! I saw a guy get his guts ripped out by two old women, right on the street! I saw another man's eyes gouged out by school children, and they made him eat them, lady; *eat them*! Have you ever seen a man eat his own eyes?"

She was numb. "No, I, uh—"

"Well, I have!" He threw a box of nails at her. "Now get to work!"

CHAPTER FOURTEEN

Barbara hefted wood, hammered. The first dozen or so minutes were trying, hell on her wrists, but the job became easier once she started to visualize each nail as an asshole in her life. Uncle Max. Aunt Clara. The guy from third grade who'd lifted her skirt with the tip of his pencil. A litany of people passed before her mind's eye, some with forgotten names and others with half-remembered faces. Then she saw herself being an unmitigated ass to them all and pounded the nails harder still. Her body felt mechanical. Nail, knock, heft; nail, knock, heft...

Barbara wasn't sure how much time had passed when she heard the man stop hammering. He stood back, surveyed his most recent handiwork. "Not bad," he said, "and it looks like we've got the most vulnerable spots in this room sealed, but we'll have to take care of the rest and do reinforcement work soon."

Barbara shook her fingers. "My hands are about to fall off. Can we relax first?"

The man considered this. "Okay. We've got some time still. Lucky for us, the major league assholes haven't found this place yet."

"Major league assholes?"

"Weren't you outside? Didn't you see?"

"I—I really don't know what I saw. It's all a blur."

"Let's take a seat," he said.

Barbara nodded, joined him on the sofa. She lit another cigarette, and the man did likewise. "You smoke, too?" she asked.

"Like a freight train."

"Well, I only have one left so, uh, could I bum a few of yours later?"

"I've got plenty of smokes. We can hot-box this place all night long."

"Oh thank god!"

He crossed his legs. "So, what's your name?"

"Barbara."

"Hello, Barbara. I'm Todd. Do you own this place?"

"No, somebody ran me off the road and—"

"Same here. Are the owners around? Have you seen them?"

She shook her head.

"Figures. They're probably assholes, too, doing god knows what." He fiddled with his cell phone. "I've tried to get a hold of others, but it's still dead." He put it away. "How about yours?"

She tried to dial her sister's number again. "Still nothing, but I saw a guy outside using one."

"Yeah, me too. How about the TV?"

"It stopped working a minute after I turned it on." Barbara then asked what she considered the most important question. "Do you know what's wrong with those…people?"

"They're assholes."

"Yeah, I got that. But—"

"Do you think I'd have let that cracker—no offense—insult my race if he weren't one of them? You've got to be careful around those bastards. You can't—"

Suddenly, something shattered outside. Barbara and Todd rushed to the window. Peeling back the curtain, they looked out. One asshole had joined another by Todd's pick-up. With rocks, they smashed the last remaining headlight.

"Fuck your truck, buddy!" taunted one.

The other mooned him, then started slashing tires.

Todd's fists tightened. "I just got those yesterday!"

"Don't stop them. Tires aren't worth it." Barbara said this, but didn't believe it. If the truck were hers, she'd be tempted to tear out the door and then tear into the two pricks until *their* headlights went out.

"You're right," Todd said. "I'll just let them have their way with Old Betsy."

"Old Betsy?"

His lower lips curled. He seemed on the verge of tears. "Yeah, that's her name, and she was my favorite."

"Her?"

He turned to face Barbara, gaze hard and unflinching. "I name my trucks, okay! That doesn't make me weird or crazy or a bad person!"

She took a step back, but Todd extended his hand quickly, a placating gesture. "Look, I'm sorry for lashing out. It's just a sore spot. Lost a few wives due to my trucks."

"Oh, okay…"

"And I'm a bit on edge now. You've got to look past me. Let's just sit back down, have another smoke, and I'll tell you everything I know."

CHAPTER FIFTEEN

Todd related his story:

"I was at Sonny's Diner, a hole-in-the-wall straight from the 50s. Probably hasn't been remodeled since then, but that's part of its charm. If shit ever blows over, you should check it out. At any rate, they serve biscuits and gravy there, even at lunch and dinner. That's the main reason I went.

"Let me tell you about those biscuits. The crust is so golden, so flaky. And the inside is fluffy like a cloud. Whenever I ate them, I could imagine myself floating, straight up to Heaven!"

"Okay, but—"

"And the gravy's to die for. Better than grandma, god rest her, used to make. The little hunks of sausage are ideally sized, perfectly seasoned, too. I believe their sausage is made locally. No frozen shit."

"Can we get past the biscuit and gravy stuff?"

"Oh, sorry. I have a thing for biscuits and gravy. Kind of like my trucks, I've lost a number of wives over them, too."

Barbara wondered, absentmindedly, exactly how many wives Todd had had, and how one might be lost over a plate of biscuits and gravy.

"Well, my waitress was being pushier than usual. Pressuring me to order even after I asked for more time because I couldn't decide on the hash browns or mashed potatoes. When I was ready, she wouldn't come back out to serve me. She served other guys, however.

"Then a whole bus load of tourists pulled up. Wasn't expecting that. Didn't seem like their kind of place. One thing I knew, however, was that a bad experience was about to get worse. Who the hell knew if I'd ever get my food?

"The bus door opened, and people kept coming out, more people than there should have been seats. I had no idea how that little diner would hold so many eaters.

"It did, but barely. Everybody's back was against everyone else's, and the new customers were pushy, demanding. They all wanted their orders *right then*. No one was in the mood to wait. They had loud conversations amongst themselves, too. Some were practically screaming. Kids kept crying, and this old lady stood right in front me, ass near my face. She wouldn't stop farting! I thought maybe she couldn't help it, but it was still a madhouse, and some regular customers got up and left. I stayed because I fucking wanted those biscuits and gravy.

"I looked for my waitress, but she was just sitting back on her ass, smoking a cigarette. A younger, prettier one had to deal with the rush. She brought food out for this guy—some expensive-looking businessman type. He declared it shit without even tasting it, called the waitress stupid and ugly and threw his plate across the room. Then he told her to go back and do things right this time.

"The waitress smacked him. I assumed she'd be fired, though I wanted to give her a high five. But she… transformed. My God, she wasn't even female anymore! She became this beer-gutted construction worker and propositioned a pretty lady. When she smacked him, she became an asshole, too, a major league one with a chainsaw and a mask that looked like human flesh.

"Then *all* the assholes stopped being rude and started getting physical. Mostly fists, but some knives and chains and nunchucks and I don't know what else. These biker guys—non-assholes—tried bashing in faces, but it did no good. Another wrapped his hands around a neck and squeezed until he couldn't squeeze anymore. A few others grabbed knives and started stabbing the more violent ones. Nobody died, but everybody who got physical with the new arrivals became assholes.

"That's when I realized how they happened—the transformations, I mean. You turn into an asshole if you're an asshole to an asshole."

"Oh crap," said Barbara.

"What?"

"Nevermind. Keep going."

"I had to get out of there, so I pushed against the people, heard their insults and felt their slaps, but I took them. I took them until I got back in my truck and saw a bunch of cheerleaders going down the sidewalk, and a guy walking up toward them. Guess he didn't know anything was wrong, because he kept going, and I watched him and thought, *run man, run*, but I just sat there, like an idiot. Should have waved. Should have screamed. Should have done *something*, because they tore into him, Barbara, and they just…walked right over his eviscerated corpse! One blew a kiss at me as she passed. I nearly gagged.

"Before, I thought cheerleaders were hot. Those little skirts and bright panties—oh boy! Now, I won't be able to see a football game again—provided there is another football game—without wanting to put a stake up every fucking cheerleader's ass I see."

"I saw a bunch of cheerleaders, too," Barbara added. "But they weren't that bad. They just—"

He slammed a fist on the table, rattling it. "All cheerleaders are bad!"

"Okay, okay! All cheerleaders are bad!"

Todd centered himself, cleared his throat. "Anyway, there was another group of assholes across the street, and they were hooting and hollering and taking pictures! At that point I knew I had to get home, lock myself up. Almost made it, too, but this drunk guy ran me off the road. Got a jolt, but didn't wreck. Then I saw this place and drove right through the grass to it.

"Now, how about your story, Barbara?"

She told it, omitting the Hare Krishna stuff, some of the more emotional elements, and the fact she was trying not to be an asshole herself at the mall. Didn't seem like the right time to bring it up. Maybe she'd never mention it.

When she finished, Todd said, "Forget black and white, I think there're only two races that have ever existed: assholes and non-assholes." He lit another cigarette.

Barbara nodded. "It makes sense."

"Yeah, tons of sense. Only now one race definitely outnumbers the other."

"But why today?"

Todd shrugged. "Who knows? Maybe things had to reach a tipping point. Once regular assholes outnumbered the good people—or even the okay or the halfway decent—those black, howling gates opened and the true assholes emerged."

Barbara felt a wave of cold travel across her. "I really don't want to think about that, Todd."

"Me, neither." He stood. "Well, we best get back to work."

Barbara's stomach rumbled. "Okay, but I'm getting pretty hungry. Mind if I take a look in the refrigerator first?"

"Don't bother. Everything's expired."

She remained dead-set on eating. "Might still be good. I've had yogurt that was three weeks past its date."

"I mean *really* expired."

"Oh."

"But I've got a sandwich in my pocket. Want some?"

"In your pocket?"

"Yeah." He withdrew it. The sandwich looked fine, almost fresh and tasty even, but it was covered in lint. She'd never seen a more lint-covered sandwich. Red lint, blue lint, green lint, purple—there were even colors for which she didn't have names.

The sight faded her hunger a bit. "That's fine. I'm okay for now."

He extended the sandwich. "You sure?" Longer pieces of lint began to sway slightly.

"Yes, very."

Todd shrugged. It amazed her when he didn't throw it away, but put it back in his pocket, perhaps to save for later.

CHAPTER SIXTEEN

Within minutes, Barbara was back to hefting and hammering. She moved a metal cabinet that stood in the way of what felt like her thousandth window. One of the drawers slid open. A filled leather holster rested inside.

"I found a gun!" She seized it, waved it in the air. "It looks like an antique—but, my god; it's loaded!"

Todd didn't turn from his work. "Remember what I just told you? You can't kill assholes with guns."

"Oh." Barbara put it back down, closed the drawer.

Finally, the living room seemed finished. Only one window remained without boards. Barbara assumed Todd would leave it, as it was so high off the ground.

They moved into a tiny, terrible-smelling bathroom, boarded the one window there and started on the adjacent bedroom. It was the sort of place a grandmother might sleep: lacy comforter, antique perfume bottles on the dresser, black and white pictures of stern-looking people—long dead—on the walls. The smell of age hung over everything. That scent reminded her of her mother's room, but she pushed the image from her mind quickly, not wanting to entertain it.

Todd glanced out the window. Eight assholes walked towards the house. Each member of the group carried oversized bags of fast food. One opened a bag and spat in it. Another noticed this and spat, systematically, into the ones he carried, too.

"Hmmm. Seems some of them got lunch for the others," Todd said. "This means they're in it for the long haul."

All the work had made Barbara forget her hunger. Now that she'd stopped, it flooded back to her. "God, I wish they'd get some for me!"

Suddenly, a face was at the window, wild-eyed and grinning. Barbara jumped back. Todd replaced the curtains quickly.

"You can't stay in there forever," the asshole screamed, "but we can wait as long as it takes!"

Barbara re-opened the curtain. "Shut up!" she screamed back at the face. "Just shu—"

Todd grabbed her, spun her around. "Barbara, relax! You're getting dangerously close to being an asshole to that asshole!"

She backed away from the curtain, shook her head and regained her bearings.

CHAPTER SEVENTEEN

Ultimately, Barbara and Todd boarded the bedroom, and then another and another still. She couldn't believe the house had so many places to sleep, and every time it seemed she'd taken care of the last window in a given room, there was another—and sometimes two or three more—that she'd somehow overlooked.

And the woodpiles kept growing. Was Todd cutting down the trees outside and rendering them for lumber? What was going on?

Barbara didn't try to answer that question. She just kept working.

Finally, mercifully, Todd shouted, "Break time!"

They reconvened back on the sofa in the living room.

Barbara felt the nicotine demon clamor for recognition. "I couldn't have a smoke, could I?"

Todd sounded almost sly. "Sure…but you could have something better, if you want." He reached into his pocket, removed a baggie brimming with fat green buds. "I got some ganja, too."

Barbara was floored. "My god, you…I mean…wow, just wow."

"I always come prepared."

She eyed the bud he'd removed and begun to separate. Clearly dank, she could smell it from where she sat.

"It's got a crazy ass name," he said, tossing seeds to the floor, "like Pink Baby Mamba Juice, or something equally stupid—but I've found the dumber the name, the better the weed." He pulled a small pipe from his other pocket. Its bowl was deep and wide.

"Pack it full," said Barbara. "As full as you can."

"Oh, I will. Just wish I had my big red bong with me. Smoking with it is a *revelation*."

Barbara imagined the bong—all tubes and chambers and holes. "I'm sure it is."

Todd left the couch, got down on a rug. Barbara joined him, sitting Indian-style. Once he finished packing the bowl, he handed her the pipe. "Take the green hit."

She lit the bowl, but coughed when the smoke reached her throat.

"It's heady," Todd said. "I'd take it easy, at least at the start."

She nodded. Tried again. This time the smoke went down smooth, and she started to feel tingles even before she could exhale. She passed the pipe to Todd. He took a massive hit, said to Barbara, "I think I'm going to check upstairs and—" but didn't have time to finish before both heard another automobile make its approach.

A black industrial-sized truck had pulled up beside the house. Something tall, covered by a tarp, sat in its bed.

"What do you think they're doing?"

"I don't know," Todd said. "Just watch."

An asshole jumped into the bed and peeled back the tarp, revealing a massive set of speakers. Seconds later, a live version of *I Wanna Rock and Roll All Nite (and Party Every Day)* penetrated and rocked the house.

Todd winced, held his ears. "I loathe KISS!"

Barbara's buzz fizzled before it could bloom. She loathed KISS, but for a very personal reason. Tommy, her childhood sweetheart, was supposed to have been at the KISS concert, but he'd stood her up that day, made her listen all alone to a band she'd paid money to see because *he* liked them. Other girls sat with their boyfriends and sucked face. Barbara sucked a cherry slurpee.

Still clutching his ears, Todd tore open a sofa cushion for the cotton. Barbara joined him, stuffed her ears, too. It did little good; the old memory gnawed at her more than the volume. It was as though the assholes somehow knew and delighted in rubbing her nose in the past.

Todd screamed to be heard over the racket. "Here, Barbara!" He extended his pipe. "A hit will take the edge off!"

She shook her head back and forth. "Nothing will take the edge off until that song stops!"

"It could be worse!"

"No, it couldn't be!" Barbara didn't elaborate her reply.

After three minutes and twenty seconds, the song ended. Less than a half-minute later, the opening chords sounded again, louder now, more bass-filled. Things on the wall shook. Glass cracked in frames.

"Fuck it!" Barbara bolted to the metal cabinet. "I'm getting the gun!"

"What?"

"You heard me!"

"No, I really didn't! Too loud!"

She clutched the weapon, caressed it. It felt right in her hand. "I said I'm going to blast holes in those goddamned speakers!"

"But isn't destroying someone else's property an asshole thing to do?"

"Maybe! Who gives a fuck?"

Todd moved in closer. "Think about it, Barbara! You might become an asshole, too!"

She walked to the one yet-to-be-boarded window in the room and opened it. "Do you want to listen to this shit until your ears bleed?"

"No!"

She took aim. "That's what I thought!"

Todd stepped back. Through the corner of her eye, Barbara watched him rifle around in a small closet. He tossed away a cane but picked up a slender black umbrella, shook it, then wielded it like a sword. She had no idea what he planned to do and, at the moment, didn't care to know. Her mind was on one thing.

She pulled the trigger. Nothing happened.

"Fucking safety!" Barbara screamed. She threw it off, let two bullets fly. The first hit the right speaker. The third went wild, lodging in a tree, but the second hit the left, and music died in the midst of a guitar solo. KISS was gone. Gone forever. Barbara savored the relative silence.

Todd watched her for almost a minute, his eyes shaded and suspicious. Then he put down the umbrella.

"So, at least from a distance, we can destroy their stuff and not become assholes. That's good to know." He smiled. "And you were quite ballsy to even try that."

Barbara wasn't sure she liked being referred to as 'ballsy,' but thanked him anyway.

"Now that's taken care of, I believe I'll look around upstairs. Maybe I'll find something useful." He paused. "Care to come with?"

"No, I'd rather just stay down here, thanks."

He cocked his head. "What? Is something bad upstairs?"

"Not bad. Just weird."

"Well, I'm going to check it out." Todd handed her the pipe. "If you want, you can nurse this while I'm gone."

Barbara wanted.

CHAPTER EIGHTEEN

Being alone with her thoughts became unpleasant quickly. Barbara got up, paced the floor, messed with her cell phone and tried the TV again. It didn't surprise her to find static on all channels.

Finally, she walked back to the window, no gun this time. Maybe the effects of the weed would render the assholes less threatening, make them seem almost funny.

There had to be at least twenty-five of them, a host of parked cars, too. Two new ones pulled up as she watched. Just below the window, a number of assholes were engaged in public sex. Still others took pictures of the copulating couples, tried to butt in, or ignored their displays entirely, preferring to mull around, trip fellow assholes, or take dumps they later smeared onto the house.

No, they didn't seem funny at all. She wanted to be mad at them, throw open the window and shake her fists and curse. At the moment, though, she felt more sorrow than rage. Marijuana hadn't had this effect on her before, but she'd never smoked it on the same day her family members had become assholes.

She sat down on the floor by the window, propping herself up with her elbows on the sill. When even that felt like too much work, she took to lying flat on the floor where she studied cracks in the ceiling that became reminiscent of familiar faces. Her brother, her mother, her sister, a thousand others… She wanted to cry.

Suddenly, Todd appeared from the kitchen. "That was fucking crazy!" He looked around. "And how the hell did I get down here?"

"I tried to tell you," Barbara replied, glumly.

He walked over to her, sat down. "What's wrong?"

"Isn't it obvious?"

He nodded. "Finally dawning on you, is it?"

"Yeah…"

"It'll be okay; everything'll work out. I promise you, on my word as an honorable man."

She continued staring at the ceiling. "How can you say that?"

"Because I have hope. Who knows? Maybe in a week everything will reverse itself. Assholes will be regular guys again, and the world will be just as we knew it."

She looked at him. "Do you believe that?"

He just offered a smile.

She sighed. "It's just…when I stop to think about it, I realize the people we knew aren't themselves anymore. If that's the case, then they're gone, and if they're gone, then they're dead."

"Their hearts didn't stop beating." He reached out, stroked her hair. "They didn't become corpses. Maybe they're just…someplace else."

Barbara pulled away from him. "Well, they're as good as dead! We can't touch them! Hear their voices!" Suddenly, she wanted very much to hear Johnny sing, if only one more time. "Do you know the Hare Krishna mantra?" she asked Todd.

"What?"

"Sorry. I guess you don't."

Todd moved in a little closer. "You're not the only person who's lost somebody. But enough bad thoughts." He cracked his knuckles. "I believe I know what will make you feel better: a nice foot rub. Always works for me."

That was perhaps the weirdest, most awkward thing to suggest. "No, I'll be okay," she said, slightly freaked out.

"Before all this shit started, people said I gave the best foot rubs in town."

"Really, I think I'll be fine."

"Are you sure?"

"Yes. 100%."

"Well, if you ever change your mind, the offer stands."

She nodded. His weird little foot rub spiel had distanced her from the more morbid thoughts. Maybe that was his intention. Displace sorrow with levity.

"Want a last hit?"

Barbara didn't like the word 'last.' "Not right now," she replied.

At that moment, something thumped against the left side of the house, then the right, then a few times against the door.

"What do you think they're doing?"

Todd listened. "I imagine they're egging the place. Probably toilet papering it, too."

"Why should we care? It's not our house."

"Must be the dumb assholes," he mused.

CHAPTER NINETEEN

They went back to work in yet another bedroom with far too many windows. There was even a window atop another window. Barbara scowled at it and cursed the architect.

Todd turned to her. "Think you could go to the basement and find more nails?"

She liked the break from hefting and nailing, but didn't want to go into the basement. It just sounded like a bad idea. Regardless, she nodded, said she'd be back in a second, climbed over piles of wood to get out of the bedroom, and then over more piles in the hallway and living room.

The basement steps were covered in cakes of bright green moss, so much so that the steps felt sodden, like her feet might plunge through a particularly rotten slat. How the hell had the homeowners—whoever and wherever they were—allowed this to happen?

Barbara tried not to think too much about it. She turned on a light at the base of the stairs, but the bulb offered little illumination. Shadowy patches and dark corners were ever present. She imagined unwelcome hands extending from them and the ghostly sound of whispered insults. She hoped she could find nails without having to venture too far from the light.

Damp and musty air irritated her nose, made her sneeze. She'd intended to get the hell back upstairs quickly, but it seemed it wouldn't be that easy. She saw planks of wood and pieces of drywall, hammers and chisels and axes and spades and shovels, everything but the one item she needed. She continued looking. With all the tools around, there simply had to be nails.

Finally, she located a cache in six rusted coffee cans on the floor by the washing machine. Barbara bent down just as a tap sounded at the small window above.

She straightened, standing on her tiptoes to see out of it. One of the shirtless frat boys knelt by the window, his position such that Barbara could almost see up his cargo shorts. He knocked on the glass and looked in, a hand shading the glare.

"Please," he said to Barbara. "I need your help."

"What?"

"You've gotta let me down there with you."

She backed away. "Hell no!"

"This isn't what you think. I—"

"No, this is *exactly* what I think! I saw what you did! You can't say that wasn't you!"

"I know! I know! And I'm sorry! I had to do all those things so they'd think I was one of them. But I'm not, I swear it!"

Barbara almost extended her middle finger, but then recalled what might happen if she did. Instead, she broke eye contact with the frat boy, grabbed all six cans of nails and hoisted them up awkwardly.

"Please, there're more assholes coming every minute, and I can't keep up the charade much longer!"

She stared at him. "You swear you're not an asshole?"

"I swear on my life!"

Barbara shook her head. "I don't believe you."

"Then I swear on my mother's life!"

She turned. "I'm going to leave now."

The asshole (boy?) adopted a prayer stance. "You've gotta believe me, or I really will become one! Come on! How would you feel if you hadn't gotten in and were stuck out here with these pricks?"

Barbara turned back to him. He had a point.

"I saw my mom and dad transform, right before my

eyes, and there was nothing I could do, so please, open the window!"

Barbara studied his face. His hurt and fear appeared genuine, and his wide eyes and round, friendly cheeks made him seem like a trustworthy guy. Had she thought about it, Barbara might have pretended to be an asshole if the door had been locked.

The frat boy pleaded, "Say you believe me now!"

She thought for a second, nodded in the affirmative.

"So let me in!"

Barbara hesitated only a second more, then moved to open the window. The handle-style latch was old, rusty and she had to tug on it before it started to move.

"Hurry! I hear them! They're coming around from the other side!"

"I'm trying, but the lock's tight!" She gave it one last tug. The lock disengaged, and the window opened.

"Oh thank you!" He started to climb through, but with difficulty, as his body was almost as wide as the space. "Thanks so much!"

"Need any help getting down?"

"No, I'll be fine." Once he'd gotten all the way through, he jumped to the floor and stood beside Barbara, looking at her, smiling. "I'm so happy," he said. "I just want to hug you!"

"Oh, okay…"

The frat boy coiled his arms around her, brought her to his chest in an uncomfortably tight hug, but he groaned and began to jerk. Barbara broke the embrace just in time to see blood bubbles erupt over his lips. A second later, his eyes became grapes as a wooden pole, draped with viscera, shot out of his mouth. Shock stole Barbara's words moments before she found a scream.

When the frat boy collapsed, she saw Todd holding a pole flush against the dead guy's ass. Then she noticed how the cargo shorts puckered, and saw the spreading red stain.

"Holy Christ, Todd! What did you do?"

"What does it look like?" he said, nonchalantly.

"No, no, no! He was a normal guy!"

"You think?" Todd kicked him over. "Look at what he was hiding."

She saw a bag, stained brown at the bottom. Apprehensively, she bent down and opened the flap. The smell hit her first.

"But it's only dog poo!" she shouted.

Todd said nothing, just looked up at the window. Finally: "Guess I'd better start boarding this up." He seemed pissed when he looked back at Barbara. "Go wait for me upstairs," he said. "There are certain things we need to discuss."

Barbara sat at the kitchen table for ten uncomfortable minutes, listening to Todd nail up the window downstairs. She closed her eyes, tried not to think of anything but that noise until it became the only sound in the world.

She returned to herself when it stopped. A few minutes later, she heard Todd's feet clump and squish up the moist steps. He came through the door, not seeming any happier and carrying two sharpened poles.

"Why did you trust an asshole?" he asked before he even took a seat. "Why?"

"I don't—I thought—"

"You can never be sure, and you can never—and I mean *never*—let your guard down! Do you understand?"

"I—I..."

"Say it! Say you understand!"

"I understand! But, really, you didn't have to kill him. What's the worst he could have done? Smear shit on my face?"

"No, make you eat it."

Barbara wanted to scream, but held it in. "That doesn't warrant a death sentence, either!"

Todd leaned in closer. "It doesn't matter if he was

72

holding shit or a hand grenade. He wanted nothing more than to make you like him!" He threw the second sharpened pole her way. "Take this. I made it for you in the basement."

She looked at the thing. "What do you want me to do with it?"

"The same thing I did, when the time comes."

"Oh god! I have to stick it—"

"Up the ass, yes. It's the only way to kill those sons of bitches. Now, I know killing them is an asshole thing to do, but, if you do it right, you won't become one."

"But—"

"No buts! You can't do stupid shit like you just did anymore! You can't give an asshole a chance. If you've got something to stick one with, stick it. Don't hesitate. Don't think *oh, this isn't a major-league asshole; I can hold out*. Just stake the ass!"

Barbara couldn't believe what she was hearing. "If I thought that way, I'd never have let you in. I'd have just said, *sorry! You're an asshole!*"

Todd was silent for a moment. "Okay, I'll grant you that."

"Then you've just made my point! How was I supposed to know?" She paused. "And how do *you* know about the butt-thing?"

"Experience."

Suddenly, it dawned on her. "That umbrella you picked up before I shot out those speakers. You were going to stick it up my ass, weren't you?"

"Only if you became an asshole."

"But that doesn't change the fact you were going to do it!"

"I'll defend you to the end, Barbara, and you know this. But as soon as you become an asshole, you'll be out like a light." He reached a hand towards her. "I only hope you'd do the same for me."

Barbara recoiled.

"Don't do that, please," he said. "I'm a gentleman. I never dreamt I'd say and do things like this, but I've been forced to adapt to our new reality. Learn from it, too.

"See, there's a part of my story I didn't tell earlier because, honestly, I wanted to shield you from it. I hoped maybe you'd never have to see me kill an asshole, or kill one yourself. That was a fantasy, a pipe dream, so now you must hear.

"It was back at the diner, when everything was going to hell. One of the assholes fell back onto a big knife one of the biker-guys held. It went right through his pants, up his ass—and it *killed him*. The biker-guy noticed this, started stabbing the other assholes there instead of in other parts like his friends. Everyone he stuck died, and he *never* changed. After seeing that, I knew how to kill them myself."

Barbara took a deep breath, exhaled. "You're absolutely sure there's no other way to stop them?"

"Absolutely."

"It has to go right up their ass?"

"Right up their ass."

"And through their mouths?"

"Well, maybe not that far. It's just additional insurance."

She resisted the urge to adopt a fetal position. "I don't have it in me to do something like that, Todd."

"But you're going to have to learn. There's a good chance you'll be sticking poles up so many asses you won't be able to see straight! You'll be the new King George, slaying the dragon!"

"I don't want to be King George!"

"Just remember what I said, and keep that pole handy. Okay? It's all I ask."

"Okay," she said, though a part of her wanted to respond with *hell no, I'll never stick a pole up another living thing's butt.*

"Good. I'm glad we had this talk." Todd arose. "There's another bedroom we've got to finish up; I'd like to be done with it before it's dark and too many more of those things get here."

"Fine," Barbara said. "But I want to know something first."

"What?"

"What did you do with the body?"

"Covered it with a blanket in a dark corner. You never have to see it again."

"Good."

CHAPTER TWENTY

As they passed the entrance to the den, the old grandfather clock started to rattle and shake slightly. It was as though something that didn't belong was where the pendulum should be.

Todd placed a hand on Barbara's shoulder. "Stay back," he said. "I'll take care of this." He moved toward the clock with cautious steps. Before he reached it, the door swung open and a hand emerged. Todd brandished his ass-ramming pole. Barbara realized, with horror, that she'd left hers in the kitchen. Horror only increased as she considered what she might have to do if she had it.

Seconds later, from the tiny space, a wan, balding and bespectacled man exited. He wore a rumpled brown suit. His face was covered in scratches. Close behind him: a woman in a creased and lopsided purple dress with poof sleeves. Around her neck were pearls so fat they nearly reached her chin. She'd gone heavy on the makeup, too, her look reminiscent of Adam Ant or late-period Darby Crash.

She adjusted her clothes, noticed Barbara and shouted, "Who the hell are you!"

Barbara stalked to her, said, "I could ask you the same question!" before realizing the tone of her voice.

Todd stepped up as well, addressed the husband. "Do you own this house?"

"No."

"Are you assholes?"

"You mean—"

"You know what I mean."

"No! Of course we're not!"

Todd leaned in closer. "Are you sure?"

76

"No, I—I mean yes!"

Knuckles were white against the pole. "Do you *swear*?"

"Yes! Yes, of course! We were on our way back from church when they ran us off the road."

Todd didn't seem convinced. "I only saw one wrecked car."

"It happened about a half-mile back."

"Trust us, we wouldn't be in this dump if it didn't happen," the woman said.

Barbara felt slightly more at ease. "So, how did you both…fit in there?" she asked.

"When you're desperate, there isn't much you can't do."

"And it's bigger in there than you'd think," the husband added. "Actually, a lot bigger."

Todd stopped brandishing the pole, but didn't set it down. "Why didn't you come out earlier?"

"We didn't know," he said. "We just heard noises and thought a bunch of assholes had gotten in."

"You should have known, just by hearing the stuff we said."

"Okay then, maybe we were scared!"

"I can understand that." Todd leaned the pole against a wall. "So, what're your names?"

"My name is Ellen."

"And I'm—"

"And that's Harold," said Ellen, quickly.

Harold grumbled. "You know I hate it when you—"

She glared at him. "Well, I already did, okay?"

"I'm Barbara," she said, feeling a bit awkward.

"And I'm Todd. Guess it's good that you're here. We could use a few extra hands boarding up this place."

Ellen looked around at Todd's handiwork. "Well, I think you should forget about a job already done and get in this clock. We wouldn't be leaving it if Harold didn't need to stretch his legs."

Todd seemed confused. He didn't speak for a few

seconds. Finally: "In the clock? Are you mad?"

"We already told you there's plenty of room. It isn't—"

"Hell, you could probably get lost in there!" Harold interjected.

"Shut up, Harold! I'm trying to talk!"

"Well, I was trying to talk, too!"

Ellen disregarded him. "Out in the open, you're sitting ducks. No one will think to open the clock. Did you even consider it before we came out?"

"Well…no."

"Of course you didn't! That's because you can't think outside the box, and because you can't do that, you'll all become assholes before the night is over!"

"If worse comes to worst, we can all get in the clock together," Todd suggested. "For now, it's best we continue boarding the house."

"I'm not going to jeopardize the perfect hiding place for a bunch of strangers! Get in now or stay out!"

Todd's hands were on his hips. "And how long exactly do you plan to spend in that clock, without a bathroom?"

"As long as it takes!"

The spots returned, redder than ever. Barbara's ears started to ring. She turned to Harold. "Dear sweet Jesus, could you shut that woman up?"

"No, uh—not really," he said. "But I could try."

"No, Harold! Don't even talk to me!"

"But Ellen…"

"If you want to stay here with these people, fine!" Stalking off, she slammed the clock's door behind her so hard it lost an hour.

"Doesn't look like she'll be much help," Todd said to Harold.

"She'll get over it. She always does."

"Well, she's wrong, and I hope you know that. No way am I boxing myself up when there's still work to be done out here."

Harold took a seat on the couch. Todd joined him, and Barbara did too, if only to be semi-sociable. "So, what brought you and your wife here?" she asked.

"We were at church, and there was a new preacher. Didn't think much of it. Maybe Bob was sick or something. But the preacher started making fun of the congregation. He even said my wife had ghastly makeup and didn't know how to dress herself!"

Todd smirked. "Are you sure he was an asshole and not just telling the truth?"

Harold ignored the comment. "A young guy in the front row stood up. He started insulting the preacher back and told him he was shaming God's house. Then the guy grabbed his head, fell to the floor. Thought he'd had a stroke or something, but, when he got up, he was an angry middle-aged Asian man! The wife and I got the hell out, of course, but things were even crazier on the streets..."

When Harold finished his story a minute or so later, Todd arose. "Get the last bedroom, Barbara, and I'll work on reinforcing the living room." He turned to Harold. "Care to help me with these boards?"

"Oh no, they look too heavy, and I probably should go back to the clock now. See how Ellen is doing."

CHAPTER TWENTY-ONE

In the hallway, Barbara saw that Todd had miscounted. There wasn't one bedroom left, but two.

Before picking up the first board, she looked out the window. The yard was considerably brighter than it should be. Then she realized the assholes had set up floodlights all around the perimeter of the house.

Whatever. Let them do their thing.

She started to work. Her arms ached, sometimes felt like rubber, but the house was nearly impregnable. Knowing that kept her hands lifting and hammering the boards.

From the living room, she heard a sudden commotion. At first, she thought assholes had somehow broken in. Quickly, however, she recognized the agitated voices of Ellen and Harold.

"I hate you!" said one.

"I hate you, too!" said the other. "I've always hated you!"

Barbara nailed harder so she wouldn't have to hear them, but the louder she got, the louder they were in return. They seemed intent on making her a part of their argument.

No, that's *exactly* what they wanted, and she wanted very much to oblige them.

Barbara threw down the hammer, advanced into the living room. Harold cringed on the floor. Ellen bopped his head, over and over again, with a rolled up magazine. Todd continued to nail boards to already boarded windows. Lots and lots of boards, it seemed. Seven planks deep in some places.

"You'll learn not to say shit like that!" Ellen screamed as Harold clutched his head. "You won't be getting back in that clock again until I'm through being furious with you, and who knows when that'll be!"

Barbara stomped up to them, fists in her pockets so it would be harder for them to break a nose or two.

Ellen's eyes bored into her. "This matter is between me and my husband!" She turned to Harold, pointed. "That dickless little bitch over there!"

Todd threw down his hammer. "Can you take this somewhere else? Like your precious clock?"

Ellen didn't acknowledge him. "Harold has intimacy issues, you know. Been that way for years."

"Ellen, could you please—"

"No, Harold, I can't!"

Barbara didn't know Harold, but it made her ill to hear him spoken to like that. Had she been so insufferable when she'd been a regular asshole? Despite herself, she spoke calmly: "Care to lay off the guy so we can get things done?"

"Think you can give me orders?" Ellen snorted, an almost animal sound. She flashed a huge diamond ring. "I'm worth more now than you'll ever be!"

Civility defenestrated itself. Barbara imagined her fingers lengthening, shooting towards the woman like darts or cannonballs, right into her eyes, into her brain and out the back of her skull, where nails, hideously extended, would drip blood and fragments of gray matter.

Suddenly, Todd was there, standing between them. "Relax, Barbara. How about a cigarette?"

"Actually, can I have two?"

"Two?"

"For both sides of my mouth."

"Sure." Todd tapped three out. "And I'll have one as well." He turned to Harold. "Want one, man?"

"I don't smoke," he said. "And I wish you'd do that outside."

"*Do that outside?*" Barbara shouted. "What the hell are you saying?"

"But I really can't handle cigarette smoke. It gives me hives."

Hearing this, she felt the need to cackle. "You want us to turn into one of those fuckers just because you'll itch, when you could go into the next room, or the basement if you wanted?" She started walking away; Todd followed. "Whatever! I'm through messing with both of you!"

Alone with Todd in one of the bedrooms, Barbara still fumed.

Todd tried to console her. "That lady back there, she's an asshole, but one of the regular ones we all had to deal with before this shit started, so she's not worth your anger."

"I'm—" Barbara paused as she heard Ellen and Harold start up again. She tuned them out. "I'm sorry for going off. I've been trying my best not to lash out all day."

"You're not alone in that, believe me."

"No, you don't get it." Barbara wondered how much she should say. Would Todd understand? Would he start to hate her? But she'd already started, so she might as well finish. "I used to be an asshole, too."

He scooted backwards on the bed. "What did you say?"

"I used to be—"

Nostrils flared. He lunged for the pole against the wall.

"No, no, no!" She raised her hands defensively. "Not that kind of asshole! The regular kind!"

"Oh…" He sat down the weapon. "So, you were once an asshole? I would have never guessed."

"I'm trying to better myself. Taking pills, too." She fished the pill case from her pocket and opened it. "The crappy thing is I only brought one with me to the mall."

"And those pills even you out?"

Barbara nodded.

"Then it's probably the worst time to have just one."

She sighed. "Tell me about it. You've got lots of cigarettes, which help, but they aren't going to last forever."

He patted his pockets. "Still got plenty left."

"That's not the point." She looked down at the floor, almost ashamed to make eye contact with Todd. "The point is, if I can't stop being an asshole to Ellen"—*who deserves it*, she wanted to add—"then there's no way I can make it if real assholes get in.

"And what if I just *think* I've started to change? What if I'm still the same old asshole I've always been?" She huffed. "If that's the case, I might as well go outside now. Wouldn't be a big change."

Todd crushed his cigarette, pulled out the pipe and took a hit. "Want one?" he asked.

"Yeah." She sucked a lungful of smoke and held it for as long as she was able.

"At least you're making an effort," Todd said, "and a good one at that. Think of all the shit you've gone through today."

"There's been a lot of shit." She handed the pipe back to Todd.

He thought for a short while. "Why not consider this your greatest possible challenge? If you can make it without once being an asshole to an asshole, then you're definitely cured."

"Fat chance of that."

"Look, you've made it this far." He took another hit, but instead of giving the pipe back to Barbara, he placed his hand atop hers. "You've just got to keep going. Never quit."

Barbara liked the warm feeling. She let his hand stay. "Some part of me wonders if this is all one big test. I mean, today of all days…"

"God fucking up the entire world just to test you? Seems like something he'd do."

Barbara looked at Todd then, *really* looked at him, and

was imagining him with his shirt off before she realized it. Stress combined with weed was affecting her, but maybe it was okay to let the harmless fantasy happen.

Did she really want to ask? Yes, she did. "I—I think I'll take that foot rub now."

"Sure thing, Barbara. Sure thing."

She removed her shoes, then her socks. Todd didn't take his eyes off her feet.

"Crinkle those toes for me," he said.

She crinkled those toes.

"I've long had a thing for the lower digits," he continued. "Can't explain it, really. Just thinking about them relaxes me, and your toes are very, very beautiful. Exquisitely formed."

"Really?"

"Nice clear nails, too." He paused. "But I hope I'm not offending you."

"No, Todd. You're not offending me at all."

"Good."

She extended her foot to him. Todd reached for it just as the door burst open and Harold plowed through. Ellen followed close behind.

"Can't you see I'm trying to get away from you?" Harold screamed to his wife. Ellen advanced as though she'd heard nothing.

Barbara retracted her foot. "God!" she shouted. "Can't you keep it in the other room!"

Ellen scowled at her. "We can fight wherever we want! It's our right as a married couple!"

"What are you even fighting over?" Todd asked.

"Never you mind!" Harold said.

"Yeah, butt out!"

"*You* butted *in*!"

Barbara grabbed her head. Her brain pulsed. They were doing this to torture her. She realized this, believed it even. Rearing up, she shouted, "Give me that pole, Todd!

Give it to me now!"

He sat on it quickly. "No!"

"I'm not going to ram it up her ass; I'm just going to beat her with it!"

"I'd like to see you try," Ellen scoffed.

Todd shook his head. "You shouldn't have left your pole behind, Barbara. I said keep it handy. But there's something you can do." He stood. "Hit *me* in the chest. As many times as it takes."

A portion of rage shifted over to confusion. "No, I can't do—"

"You *will!* You're not being an asshole if I give you permission!"

It *was* a tempting offer. "Are you…sure?"

He unbuttoned his shirt halfway. Barbara marveled briefly at his well-defined pectorals. They were just how she'd imagined them. "Very sure," he said. "Give me all you've got."

She stepped over to him. Confusion fell away and anger consumed it. Her spine felt electric. She no longer saw Todd standing there, but Ellen in her funky dress and makeup. She'd ruffle that dress. She'd smear that makeup. Oh yes.

And so she pounded him, just like a stress doll, her fists eventually connecting with almost every square inch of his chest. Through it all, he stood firm, never winced.

"Feel better now?" he said when she finally fell to the floor, red-faced and breathing heavily. By that time, Ellen and Harold had taken their argument into the hall.

"Yes. Much better. Thank you."

"We've got to bring them together somehow," Todd said after Barbara had composed herself.

"Or throw them out," she suggested.

"I'm not happy about this either, but if we can get

them to shut up and work with us, we improve our survival odds." He stood from the bed. "I'm going to call a meeting."

Barbara shrugged. "Well, if you want to give it a try…"

CHAPTER TWENTY-TWO

Prior to the meet-up, Todd had a heart-to-heart with Harold. Ellen had wanted to join them, but Todd refused her request. She sat on the sofa, pissed, waiting for proceedings to begin, though it was clear she had little interest in them.

Todd loomed over Harold. "Listen, I hate to even ask this," he said, "but I've got to." He looked hard at the man. "Are you sure your wife isn't an asshole?"

Harold fiddled with his collar, appeared uncomfortable. "She's always been like that. It's not...*irregular*. She's been a little testier today, sure, but we're all under a lot of stress."

"So, this isn't anything weird?"

"No, not really."

Todd's voice adopted an edge. "Man, are you *sure* your wife isn't an asshole?"

He seemed to think. "Is it possible to become one without changing form?"

"Earlier, I would have said no. Now, I'm not so certain."

"Well, she really isn't. I swear. Just don't kill her or anything, please."

Todd was silent for a while. "I won't—for now. But tell me one more thing before we go."

"What?"

"Why stick with a woman like that?"

Harold shrugged. "Maybe because she gives me the time of day."

"You can't do better?"

"Look at me. I'm not exactly a chick magnet."

"That's because you don't believe you're one." Todd tapped his head. "9/10th of sexiness is in the brain. Listen, if we make it through this, I'll teach you how to be sexy.

Hell, I'll make you the sexiest motherfucker on the planet!"

"You mean that?"

"You'll be a man's man, but only if you can stop arguing—just until we get out of this—and convince your wife to do the same. It'd be nice if you could help out a bit, too."

"Well, I guess I could nail up a few boards..."

Todd smiled. "Do that, and the deal is set."

Harold sat with Ellen on the sofa, wife on one end and husband on the other. They didn't make eye contact. Barbara sat in an armchair in an opposite corner.

Todd paced the floor in front of them all. "If we're going to make it past the night, we've got to work as a team, and if we're going to work as a team, we can't go around yelling and hitting each other."

Ellen elbowed Harold when he got too close to her.

"So listen up. This is important information. If you ignore it, you do so at your own peril."

Ellen yawned. "Go ahead, say a bunch of shit we already know."

"You just think you know everything, lady." Todd glared down at her. "Tell me, how does one become an asshole?"

She shrugged. "One of them bites you, I guess."

"Wrong! You become an asshole when you act like an asshole in front of one." He turned to Harold. "And do you know how to stop them?"

"Blast a hole in their skulls? That'd probably work."

Todd shook his head. "The only way to stop an asshole is to kill an asshole, and the only way to kill an asshole is take a big stake—or hell, anything strong enough to penetrate a pair of pants with a good shove—and send it straight up his or her ass!"

"That's ghastly!" Harold said.

Ellen looked around the room, first at her husband, then at Todd, then at Barbara. "Doesn't sound too bad to me. I feel like staking you all right now!"

"This isn't what we need, Ellen." Todd leaned in closer. "Not if we want to live."

"Well, *I* want to live," Ellen said. "But nobody else seems to want the same."

"What do you mean?"

"If you did, you'd join me in the clock."

Todd's forehead vein became visible. "Enough about that fucking clock!"

"I'm still willing to let you assholes in." She looked at Harold. "That includes you, of course."

"Could you lay off me?" He punched her from across the seat.

She punched him back.

Todd sighed.

CHAPTER TWENTY-THREE

Ellen and Harold's words had dissolved into petty squabbles that sounded more hen-like than human, and Barbara had no interest in listening anymore. Todd saw her leave, but didn't say anything or try to stop her. He probably understood it was for the best.

Through the downstairs rooms, Barbara wandered aimlessly, stopping to look at porcelain bird sculptures, angel figurines and various other things that wouldn't have attracted her attention on an ordinary day.

When she happened upon the ballerina-shaped music box again, she turned it on. The music it made was evocative, soothing, though she didn't recognize the tune. When the song ended, she rewound the box, listened again and focused hard on the melody. If she closed her eyes, she could imagine she was far away—both in distance and time—and that the music wasn't coming from a ballerina-shaped box, but a mobile hanging above her crib, and she was about to take a nap.

After a third listen, Barbara walked away, brushing one of the dozen or so interior wind chimes with her fingers. She left the living room, entered the hall and one of the many bedrooms. Maybe it was wrong to hide herself from everyone, but, at the moment, it felt right.

She closed the door behind her, took a seat on the floor between the nightstand and the bed. For a minute or two, it was nice—all silent and alone—no Ellen, no Harold. Then silence became oppressive.

Those assholes were out there, just behind the wall. She listened and thought she heard the sound of shuffling, of things scooting around. Suddenly, it seemed as though hands were slapping against the siding outside.

She tried concentrating on the things in the room, but found no solace. The boards on the windows appeared as sturdy as slats of balsa wood. The closet door seemed to sway slightly, and there was a sound like papers crunching. She doubted papers crunched themselves.

And did a shadow just dart into the bathroom?

She shook her head, made a concerted effort to think clearly. These things were nothing. Just fear playing games with her. But anything could be happening outside; the outside could come in at any time.

She heard footsteps, apparently real this time. Though she realized it had to be Todd, Barbara went a little cold before the hammering started.

She thought she'd better help him, so she stood, reentered the hall. It was definitely longer than before. The house had to contain at least two extra bedrooms now.

Damn it to hell!

She followed the noise to Todd. He was busy securing a board, but turned when he heard her approach.

"Didn't work out between Ellen and Harold, I guess," she said.

He shook his head. "They're back in the clock now."

Barbara picked up a board, the first of many, she assumed. "And they can stay there for all I'm concerned."

Hours seemed to pass. Barbara was surprised she was still able to board. Maybe prior Yoga classes had increased her stamina. She just regretted punching out the instructor last year, dropping the class and replacing it with TV.

Soon, Barbara could barely feel her hand. "Can we rest a bit?" she asked.

"Got to keep going," Todd said. "The later it becomes, the bolder these assholes will get."

"But aren't these windows secure enough already?"

"They'll never be secure enough."

She regarded the work they'd done. "But there're so many layers. They'd have to be really strong to break through them all."

"Maybe, but we'll need to put up layers and layers still. We'll need to exhaust all the wood in this house and then, somehow, find more."

"But how long before it turns absurd, Todd?"

"After twenty layers? Forty layers? I don't know, and it doesn't matter. We've got to keep boarding. It's our best hope."

Barbara looked down at her left hand. It was red, like a claw. "But I don't think I can keep doing this much longer."

Todd thought for a minute. "You've done your work," he said. "Rest now."

"Really?"

"Yeah, really. Take some time off. I can handle this."

Though Todd was a strong, well-proportioned man, she saw obvious traces of fatigue in him. Legs and arms shook slightly; his shoulders slumped.

"Seriously, Todd. I can—"

"No, I mean it."

Barbara turned to walk out the door but, at that moment, heard a grunt and a clatter, and Todd cursing beneath his breath. She spun around quickly.

"Don't worry." He bent at the waist, clutched his knees. His eyes were red, but he hadn't smoked in over an hour. "It's just my back."

"Todd, please rest, too."

"Not yet, Barbara. I'll be fine."

"If you insist," she said, reluctantly.

"I do." Then he resumed nailing.

CHAPTER TWENTY-FOUR

At the entrance to the living room, Barbara was surprised to see Ellen and Harold outside the clock. She considered reversing her course, but instead entered the room and sat in a chair directly opposite them. She knew Ellen would say something tart later if she dared turn away now.

Barbara hoped the two were making amends, though Ellen thumbed through a magazine and Harold looked down at nothing. She found letting her mind wander preferable to dwelling on the couple. Her thoughts skipped to random things: a particularly nice Italian meal she'd eaten months ago, a show on TV she used to like, a song she'd heard only once but somehow remembered...

"Like what you see?" Ellen asked.

Barbara's daydream world crumbled. "What?" she said.

"You were staring."

She didn't realize she'd been doing that. "Oh, sorry."

"Well, you were."

"I said I was sorry."

"Sure, but you didn't mean it."

Barbara wanted to bite her tongue, but the will was lacking. "What's your problem, anyway?" she asked. "Why don't you just stay in the clock? Earlier, you said we couldn't join you if we didn't go *right then*—yet here you sit!"

"What can I say? It's a little more comfortable here."

"Don't you think that's—"

"I really don't have to explain myself or my motivations to you."

"Okay, sure. You don't. Just go on with your hypocritical little—"

Barbara fell silent. Her stomach had called up to her in a way she hadn't heard in years. Sounded like a cave echo.

93

"Excuse you," Ellen said.

Barbara ignored the woman as her stomach groaned a second time. Wasn't surprising; a full day had passed since she filled it last. She tried to think of something other than consumption, but couldn't. If only she could eat. Didn't have to be a full-course meal. Just *something*.

Like a bite of Ellen's candy bar.

Barbara's subconscious mind had honed in on the bar ahead of her conscious one. The woman had brought it from her purse and now tore at the wrapper.

Barbara considered her words. "I, uh, couldn't have some of your candy bar, could I?"

Ellen took a bite. "No."

"Come on, just a little. We don't have to love each other afterwards."

"It's already got my germs on it."

Spots returned. "Germs don't spread all the way down the bar, Ellen."

"Mine do." She took a second bite, much larger than the first.

Barbara willed away the spots. She saw the field, instead. "I haven't eaten in a long time. Please, I—"

"You'll just shit it out later," Ellen huffed.

"You will, too!"

Harold looked up from the seat he was staring at. "Come on, don't be a bitch," he said to his wife. "Just give her a piece."

She turned to him. "What did you say?"

"You heard me, Ellen."

Squabbling started anew. Barbara stood, walked away from it before a Technicolor murder-fantasy could start playing in her mind. She'd just try the refrigerator. She remembered what Todd had said, but maybe his definition of *expired* was more stringent than her own.

Barbara entered the kitchen, opened the refrigerator door.

The smell that burst forth was curdling. She held her nose as she marveled at bushes and trees and vines of colorful mold that grew wild in the compartment, a mini-forest. It was impossible to tell what the stuff had once been, though BEST IF USED BY JUNE 14, 1982 was visible on one package.

Barbara closed the door, returned to the bedroom where Todd still worked. She couldn't believe she was about to ask him this:

"Could I please have some of your sandwich?"

"You look peaked." Todd reached into his pocket, tossed the sandwich to her. "Take it all."

A few minutes later, Barbara sat at the kitchen table, linty sandwich on a cracked porcelain plate she'd found above the counter, a glass of water—the only thing to drink—to its left. Ellen had laughed when Barbara carried the sandwich past her, but Barbara said nothing and kept going.

Maybe Ellen had been right to laugh. Barbara frowned as she picked at the thing. Its meat seemed drier now, the lint, longer and fuzzier, almost sweater-like. She tried scraping it away. It returned as though attracted magnetically to the bread.

But she had to eat—no choice—so she closed her eyes, opened her mouth and bit down. She swallowed hard, gagged. Still, she managed to finish almost a quarter of the sandwich before barfing into the sink.

Todd popped his head into the kitchen. "Did you like the sandwich?" he asked.

Barbara wiped the last remaining trace of throw-up from her lips. "Yeah, it was great."

In the living room, Ellen continued to enjoy her candy bar.

CHAPTER TWENTY-FIVE

Suddenly, there was a crash.

Barbara ran from the kitchen into the living room. She saw Ellen and Harold first. No longer on the couch, Ellen gasped and pointed. Harold stood behind her, clutching her shoulders, using her like a shield.

Barbara looked to a window. Three arms had broken through the boards. Assholes outside began moaning—a horrible, monstrous sound.

"Oh god!" Harold shrieked. "They're going to get in!"

There were thudding footsteps in the hall. Todd rushed into the living room, a board still in his grip. "What's happening!" he shouted.

"Just fucking look!" shot Ellen.

Todd ran, and Barbara followed suit, but before they could reach the nearest arm, the moaning stopped and all hands waved.

"Just foolin'!" said the assholes as one.

"Yeah," continued a single voice. "No need to invade now. We're just hanging out and having fun until supplies arrive."

"What do you mean—" Ellen started.

"I wasn't talking to you, bitch."

"We're keeping you on your toes, that's all," said a deeper voice. The arms began to pull out. "See you again soon…"

CHAPTER TWENTY-SIX

Todd had started nailing replacement boards over areas where arms had entered, but the new boards, though sturdy, weren't as secure as those that had been lost. Barbara offered assistance. Ellen and Harold sat watching them on the sofa.

As Barbara returned from the other side of the room, boards in hand, she glanced over at Ellen and noticed the folded candy bar wrapper that protruded from her pocket. Perhaps it was best to say nothing, to just let it go, but her mouth opened before her brain told it to do otherwise.

"Why didn't you throw away the wrapper?" Barbara asked. "Saving it as a souvenir?"

She turned, stared at Barbara. At least ten seconds passed before she spoke. "I'm not finished with it, and if I didn't have it in the wrapper, it would get all linty." She smirked. "Like the sandwich you ate."

Just move on. Go back to Todd. See how he's doing, she thought. Rather, she said, "I don't see why you wouldn't give me a little piece. Just something, you know. We're both human here."

Ellen shook her head. "Sorry, I don't give handouts."

"I'm not a beggar! Just someone who hasn't eaten all day!"

"Same difference," Ellen huffed. "Besides, I'm saving the rest for my daug—"

Barbara felt her eyes widen. "What did you say?" she asked, though she already knew the answer.

Todd had heard, too. He stopped work, walked over to Ellen and Harold. "Your daughter?" he said. "You never mentioned a daughter."

"I, uh—" Harold fumbled.

Barbara had the couple on the defensive. She savored this fact, pressed on. "And why didn't she come out with you?"

"It's because she's an asshole." Todd stated, matter-of-factly.

"No, that's not what I'm saying!" Harold shrieked.

"Then what exactly *are* you saying?"

Ellen boxed her husband. "Harold, shut up and let me talk!" She turned to Todd, glared. "Harold's an infant in man's clothes. He gets scared easy, but I don't. You can threaten me all you like, but you're not going to threaten my daughter. She's no asshole. She's sick and can't be around other people, especially fuckers like you!"

The insult didn't seem to faze Todd. "Okay," he said. "Just bring her out so I can see."

"What?" Ellen cried. "You want me to parade around a sick girl for your amusement? Hell no!"

"Then we're going in and getting her."

Ellen shot up from the couch. "Over my dead—"

Todd aimed his ass-ramming pole at her. "Okay. Whatever it takes."

CHAPTER TWENTY-SEVEN

It was dark inside the narrow hall of the clock, dank and chilly. Moisture dripped from walls like those in a cave. Echoing footsteps sounded hollow. Todd and Barbara held out lighters that illuminated nothing ahead but more darkness.

"Where is she?" Todd asked.

"A bit farther up. We hid her in a cubbyhole," said Harold. Ellen said nothing.

Suddenly, Barbara felt the presence of wind, blowing from her left side. She swung the lighter around, saw the mouth of what appeared to be a huge cave and assumed it was where Ellen and Harold had hid.

Minutes later, Harold stopped. "Here," he said, pointing at darkness.

Todd re-ignited his lighter. A hole in the wall was revealed. Deep inside it and almost hidden in a corner: a burlap sack that seemed filled with something human.

"That's our daughter," Harold said. "She's in there, I mean."

Todd looked askance at Harold. "Kind of big for a young girl, don't you think?"

"Well, Anna's always been a bit frumpy and a little—"

Ellen smacked the words out of her husband's mouth.

"And why isn't she moving?" Barbara asked. "And why is she in a sack?"

"Because of her medication! Because she's cold and she's asleep and you're disturbing her!"

"Drag her here," Todd said to Ellen. "I want to see."

"No! You have no right to order me around, or even look at my daughter!"

"He has every right if she's an asshole," Barbara said.

"I'm telling you, she's not! She's just a very sick girl!"

Todd was resolute. "Then why conceal her from us? Maybe we could have helped."

"*Could have helped*? Look at what you're doing now and tell me why we didn't tell you! Your idea of helping is backwards as shit!"

Todd seemed to realize he wouldn't get much out of Ellen. He turned his attention to Harold. "Be upfront with me. Is your daughter an asshole?"

"I—uh, well. No, I—"

Todd reared his hand back. "You'd better—" But then he stopped. "Listen," he said, suddenly quiet. "Do you hear that?"

Barbara turned left, turned right. "Hear what?"

"Shhhh."

She fell silent, listened. Something *was* up ahead, making muted rustling sounds, and maybe gentle footsteps, too.

Todd turned to Ellen and Harold. "Are you hiding anyone other than your daughter in this clock?"

Harold stammered, "I don't think—uh—"

Todd leaned into him. "*Are you hiding anyone else?*"

Harold lifted his arms as though to push Todd. Instead, hands shook in the air. "No! No, we're not!"

Todd leaned back. "That's all you needed to tell me."

"Sorry, but I'm nervous! Fucking nervous, okay!"

"Whatever." Todd pointed at the burlap wrapped thing on the floor. "I'll give you a pass for now, but if your daughter *ever* comes out of this clock, and she isn't who you said she is, I'll use the pole." He gripped it for emphasis. "Are we clear?"

Harold nodded almost imperceptivity.

"I'm serious; no joke. But now we've got to find out what's making those sounds."

"Can I wait back in the—"

"Don't be a pussy, Harold," said Ellen.

CHAPTER TWENTY-EIGHT

The darkness inside the clock remained unbroken. The space grew tighter and tighter until everyone walked a single-file line, with Todd at its head. No one spoke, and the cave-like silence began to weigh heavily on Barbara. She imagined walls closing in on her, squeezing her, crushing her bones. She wanted a cigarette, but didn't dare light one.

"Hear that?" Ellen said. Barbara jumped a little.

"Yeah, definitely footsteps," Todd replied. "Sounds like they're coming from behind something."

They continued walking until it seemed that the hall terminated in a dead end. It wasn't until they were almost upon it that they recognized yet another grandfather clock, flush with the wall.

Todd put his ear to its door. "I don't hear anything anymore."

"Maybe they've heard us, too," Barbara whispered.

"Maybe..." He kept listening.

"What are you waiting for? Go ahead, open it!" Ellen said, reaching past Barbara to push Todd's back.

"Give him time!" Barbara snapped.

"Get your pole ready, Barbara," Todd said. "Ellen, Harold, you shouldn't cross until I say it's safe."

Harold sighed with relief.

"I can cross whenever I please," said Ellen.

Todd grumbled, but said nothing more. He reached out, seized the small brass knob and turned it.

The door opened with a prolonged squeal. Barbara winced. Todd stepped first into yet another chamber, equally dark but apparently vast. Stalactites hung from the ceiling. Bioluminescent mold clung to walls as water

101

droplets fell into pools and echoed.

"Anyone here?" Todd shouted.

Barbara didn't breathe while she waited, listened. Seemed like half a minute passed before she exhaled. "Maybe we just imagined it," she said, just as something big came at them from a short distance. It resolved itself rapidly: a football player, replete in stark white uniform and helmet.

"Stake it, Barbara!" Todd screamed. "Stake its ass!"

"But I—I can't!"

His voice was a fierce roar. "You can and you will!"

In a second, the football player would be upon her. Barbara closed her eyes, muttered a quick, directionless prayer and spun to the left. Now facing the player's back, she didn't think, just sent the pole traveling in an arc with as much force as she could muster.

The guy collapsed on the floor, cursing, holding his ass. But Barbara knew the pole had not gone up it. If anything, it had just penetrated his left cheek.

"He's not dying!" Harold shrieked.

"That's because I fucked up!" Barbara collapsed as well. A few moments of mental chaos, then she accepted her fate and flopped over, stomach on the floor, butt in the air. Todd would have a clean shot when the time came.

Her head titled to the left. She saw Todd rush the football player. It seemed like a scene from a movie that no longer interested her. The actor who'd been Todd kicked the guy over, planted a foot on his back. "Don't watch this if you can't handle it," he said, maybe to Ellen, maybe to Harold; Barbara didn't know or care. Then he raised the pole over his shoulder.

"Stop!" screamed a small feminine voice, somewhere in the darkness. "He's not one of them!"

"Who's that?" Todd pointed the stake outwards. "Who's talking?" Ellen scrambled in the direction of the sound. Todd looked down at the football player and seemed to consider his options. Looking back at the pole, he frowned, turned away and followed Ellen.

As both disappeared in the blackness, Barbara realized she felt no pain. She reached up to touch her face. The contours were familiar. If transformation were eminent, shouldn't she have experienced *something* already?

Nevertheless, she remained on the floor for a few seconds more, listening to the noise of things she could not see:

"…an asshole?"

"No! …swear to…"

"…are too!"

"…not!"

"…hole and you know…"

"…stake her!"

Barbara embraced good fortune, stood and stepped around the still cursing and moaning football player.

As she neared the commotion, she saw a young woman in a cheerleader's outfit, curled tightly in a corner, trembling. Todd and Ellen loomed over her like angry giants. Todd's face—troll-like, scrunched in rage—disconcerted her most of all.

"Who are all you people!" the cheerleader asked upon spotting Barbara. "A bunch of assholes?"

Todd glared at her. "Barbara's no asshole! *You are!*"

Ellen turned to Barbara, smirked. "Looks like Todd and I finally found something we agree on."

Below them, the cheerleader seemed ready to bolt.

"No, you don't fucking move!" Todd jabbed his ass-ramming pole at her. "I know your type; you just stay right where we can all see you!"

She coiled her legs beneath her. "*My type?*"

"Yeah," Todd spat. "Fucking cheerleaders!"

The situation was deteriorating rapidly. Something had to give. Moving closer to Todd, Barbara put her hand on his shoulder. "I think maybe you should relax and—"

"No!" he roared, and Barbara, stunned, took a few steps back. Behind her, in the darkness, the football player moaned louder.

"Could you fucking stop that?" Todd shouted.

"…my ass… my ass," the football said, his first discernable words.

Todd returned his attention to the cheerleader. "If you're not an asshole, then why are you dressed like one?"

"I'm not dressed like an asshole! I'm dressed like a cheerleader!"

"Same difference."

Ellen butted in. "So, why aren't you in normal clothes now? I sure don't see a stadium in this clock!"

"Because shit went down in the middle of the game! I didn't have time to change! All I could do was get the hell out of there!"

"Football season is over," Todd said.

"It was a special exhibition game! For charity! For kids who—"

"Likely story," Ellen huffed.

"But it's true! Look! Look!" said the cheerleader. "I—I got photos in my purse!" She took out a billfold, presented it to Todd. "See! It's me!"

Ellen came up to Todd, whispered in his ear. "If assholes change clothes when they transform, it only makes sense that their identification would change, too."

Todd nodded. His fingers tapped against the pole.

"We're not assholes!" the football player shouted.

"Shut up, asshole!" Todd screamed over his shoulder.

The player repeated the statement, but his voice broke, sounded pained. He was moaning again in seconds.

"Don't listen to him," Ellen said. "Ram her, Todd. Then ram her jock boyfriend."

He licked his lips. "Yeah, I'm going to ram them."

Again, Barbara approached Todd. "Really," she said, this time more adamantly, "you don't want to ram somebody who might not be—"

"Go away, Barbara!"

She grabbed his shoulder, almost succeeded in spinning him around. "Hear me out, please!"

He reared back, looked ready to strike her. Barbara ducked, but he relaxed his hand, breathed in and out. "Okay, what?" he said.

"If you stake non-assholes, it's murder. And there's no bigger asshole than a murderer."

"But look at her!" He pointed; the girl cringed at his attention. "Can't you see what she is?"

"You can't let something in the past—"

"*In the past?* That was a few hours ago!" His eyes went wild. "I still see the blood!"

She clutched his shoulders tighter. "Look at me, Todd! I'm still here! Doesn't that prove they're human?"

He tried to pull away; Barbara held on. "What are you talking about?" he said, finally.

"I missed that guy's asshole, but I didn't change!"

He fell silent for a moment. "Maybe things are different this time. Hell, Barbara, I'm no expert on this shit!"

"And you told that football guy to *fucking stop*! Then you called him an asshole!"

His response was perfunctory. "Guess it wasn't strong enough to change me."

"But—"

"No! It only proves I need to police myself better."

Another approach seemed in order. "How about you and Ellen sit back and let me try to talk with the girl," Barbara said. "Okay?"

He said nothing.

"Come on, Todd."

After a few more seconds of silence: "Go ahead, talk with her if you must. But be careful, and don't blame me if anything bad happens."

Barbara knelt beside the girl and tried to make eye contact. The girl looked away quickly. Her bottom lip quaked.

"What's your name?" Barbara asked.

"Linda," she said, so low Barbara had to assume she'd heard right.

"Well, my name is Barbara, and I want you to know something."

"K-know what?"

"I don't think you're an asshole, and I don't think your boyfriend is, either." Barbara looked towards the football player. She could barely see him, but it seemed he'd finally sat up. "He's your boyfriend, right?"

She nodded in the affirmative. "His name is Billy."

"Well, sorry for staking Billy. But you do understand?"

She said nothing.

"I don't think I hurt him too bad. If we can convince Todd and Ellen you're not assholes, he'll be fine."

"What's wrong with that man? Why is he so, so—"

"He had a bad cheerleader experience."

She seemed confused. "Did one stand him up?"

"Not actual cheerleaders. Assholes."

"Oh."

"But Todd's not a bad guy. He's a very good guy. Just wait, you'll see."

She titled her head a bit, looked past Barbara's left shoulder. "Who's that other woman?"

"Ellen," Barbara said, and left it at that.

"Is she your—"

"No, she has absolutely nothing to do with me."

"But—"

"Enough about Ellen!" Barbara saw fear blossom again in the girl's eyes. "It's okay, it's okay," she said calmly. "Why don't you just try to relax and tell me how you got here?"

"I, uh, guess I could—"

"He's trying something!" Ellen shouted suddenly.

"Look, Todd! Look! He's trying something!"

"Hold on," Barbara said to the girl. "I'll be right back."

"No, don't leave me. Stop—"

"Do you want your boyfriend staked, for real this time?"

The girl shook her head.

She turned again. "Then let me go."

In a corner, crouching like the cheerleader, Harold was barely visible. His wife shrieked and pointed as Todd maintained a defensive stance, pole out and eyes fixed on the football player's ass. It seemed he was waiting only for the guy to move.

"Oh god," Barbara said. "What's going on?"

Ellen continued to point. "He was reaching for something behind his back!"

"I was reaching for my ass because somebody put a hole in it!" he screamed.

Barbara looked down at the football player; guilt gnawed at her. "That somebody was me," she said. "And I'm sorry. I thought you were an asshole."

"Thought?" Ellen shouted. "He is! They both are!"

"Then why haven't *you* transformed?" Barbara turned to Todd. "You, too."

Again, he seemed to consider things; his posture relaxed slightly. "She might be—"

"Oh, don't let her win you over, Todd!"

"I said she *might* be right." He looked back towards the cheerleader, grimaced, but lowered the pole. "Still, I don't feel very good about this."

"Give me the pole, then! If you can't do it, I will!"

Barbara slapped away her grasping hand. "Give it a rest, Ellen!"

"You know we have to!"

"No, Barbara's right. We can't stake them until we

know for sure."

Ellen groaned.

"Just leave," Barbara said. "Tend to your *daughter*." She considered adding *you hypocritical whore*, but decided against it.

"Okay, fine!" She pointed at the cheerleader. "But that bitch is an asshole, I promise you!" With that, she stormed out and slammed the clock door behind her.

"No, lady," Barbara said as the bang echoed through the chamber. "You're the bitch."

CHAPTER TWENTY-NINE

Five emerged from the clock. Barbara headed the line, followed by Linda and Billy. Todd walked just behind the wobbling football player, glaring intermittently at his ass. Harold took up the rear.

Ellen sat on the sofa on the other side of the room. She arose when she saw the others exit, walked silently past them and reopened the door to the clock.

"Honey, no! Come back!"

She stepped inside.

Harold darted back through the door before it could close. Muted squabbling ensued almost instantly.

"I don't think I'm welcome here," Linda said to Barbara.

"Don't mind Ellen," Barbara replied. "Just try to forget—"

"You're *not* welcome here," Todd interjected. "Not yet."

Billy's hands were still on his ass. "Can we do *anything* to prove we're not assholes!"

"Don't know," said Todd. "But I do know that I want both of you to stay in my sight. Don't even think of splitting up or wandering into other rooms."

"Todd, haven't we—"

He held up a hand. Barbara fell silent. "Barbara and I are going to the living room. We're going to fix some windows there and you're going to sit on the couch. Maybe we'll talk off and on; get to know one another, see how human we are."

"But I can't sit!" Billy cried.

"I gotta help him," Linda pleaded. "Can't we just go to the bathroom and—"

"No!" Todd shot back. "The last thing I want is you two alone together!" He turned to Barbara and spoke in a softer tone. "You'll have to tend to him."

"Me! But—"

"And don't forget your pole," he continued.

"I'm not sure I want another woman looking at my boyfriend's ass!" Linda exclaimed.

"Not my problem." To Barbara, he said, "Meet me and the cheerleader in the living room when you're done."

"Sorry about this," Barbara said to Linda before she helped Billy into the bathroom, bent him over the commode and pulled down his pants. Linda had just nodded as she took a forced seat on the couch.

Barbara knelt by the football player's ass, a mere eight inches from her face. He had kept his helmet on, and, though weird, it was somewhat easier on her that way. She could imagine he didn't have a face or a brain under there, that he was just a butt, a lump of football clothes and underwear.

Barbara looked only at the hole she'd made. "It's not even as bad as I thought," she said. "In a few days, you probably won't feel a—" She stopped, considered her words. Would they even have a few days? Starting anew, she said, "Really, this isn't that big of a deal."

"You think?" For the first time since his near impalement, Billy wasn't shouting or moaning. His natural speaking voice: deep and husky.

"Yeah, but it's going to take a little work." She went to the medicine cabinet, removed a bottle of peroxide, some gauze and a bandage. Kneeling again, she poured the peroxide. It bubbled, foamed and turned pink with blood.

"Oww! That burns!"

"I know," Barbara soothed. "But it'll be over soon." Those words, she quickly realized, might have been poorly chosen, too.

After the fizzing stopped, she patted his left cheek dry

and began to dress the wound. From the living room, she heard hammering start up. No raised voices or screams or squishy, popping sounds, though. She took that as a positive sign.

"Sorry you have to see this," Billy said.

Barbara was taken aback. "I should be the one to apologize."

"No, I get it. I mean, I was pissed at first, but I can't blame you. Hell, I thought you were one of them, too."

"Well, at least it didn't go all the way up. I don't know what I'd do if I'd done that."

He nearly laughed. "Me neither."

In the living room, Barbara was surprised to find Todd working alongside the cheerleader. He seemed tense, ill at ease, and paused to look over at the girl.

Barbara assumed this had been Linda's idea. Nevertheless, it relieved her, and she joined them by the window. Just as she grabbed some nails, she heard hammering start on the opposite side of the room. It was the football player, nailing up boards, too.

"Billy!" Linda said. "You should rest!"

He shook his head. "Nah, I was just being a big baby. It's not that bad."

"Are you sure?"

"I'm positive."

And so they continued lifting and hammering and nailing. Todd's tension fell away gradually. In time, he focused only on the job at hand, as did everyone else, working like four machines moving from window to window, room to room.

CHAPTER THIRTY

When it came time to rest, Todd brought a couch from across the room closer to the one in the center to accommodate the new arrivals and Harold, who had just stepped out of the clock, sans Ellen.

"You're a very pretty lady," Harold said to Linda, seconds after they both sat down.

"Thank you," she replied

"How old are you?"

"Billy and I"—she emphasized her boyfriend's name—"we're both 19."

"19! What a wonderful age! I remember when I was 19. Teenagers are so free," he mused.

She sounded a little uncomfortable. "Yeah, I, uh, guess we're...free."

"Well, you shouldn't let that freedom slip away like I did. You should embrace it and just do, well, whatever comes natural."

"Okay," she said, "but with all those assholes out there, we can't do much."

Todd unleashed a protracted sigh that was lost on Harold. He leaned in closer to Linda. "You know, I never thought you were one of them." A pause. "Well, maybe I did for a second, but only for a second."

Barbara tried to get a word in. "So, are you both—"

"I don't think an asshole could ever be as pretty as you. Really, you look...just great." He lifted his hand as though to touch her, but noted Todd's glare and put it down quickly. "Your boyfriend, he's a very, very lucky man."

Barbara turned to Billy. It has hard to tell, seeing that he still wore the helmet, but she imagined he was seething.

Why couldn't Harold have stayed in the clock? At that moment, she had an idea how to get him back in.

"Hey, Todd," she shouted over Harold. "Think you can throw me a smoke?"

"With pleasure," he said.

Barbara caught it in the air, lit it and blew a gray cloud straight to Harold.

He threw up his hands. "Oh god, not more smoke! I told you I can't handle smoke!"

"Then go away!"

Harold looked flustered for a second, then uncertain, then almost scared. "O—okay," he said. "It's my turn to check on my daughter anyway."

"You go do that," Todd told him.

He arose quickly. "I'm sorry if I offended you, Linda. But you really are—"

"Just go!" shouted Billy.

Turning, the man scampered out of the living room and to the clock.

"Can you believe that guy?" Linda said once Harold was out of earshot. "God, how creepy!"

"I should have done something," Billy said. "But I—I was afraid I might become an asshole."

"Harold's not that kind of asshole," Barbara assured him.

"I know, but—" His words trailed away. He looked down at his hands as though they'd failed him.

"It's okay, Billy." Linda rubbed his shoulder. "It wasn't as though he was groping me."

"Maybe not with his hands…"

"Well," said Todd. "When you're stuck in a strange place, surrounded by assholes, you just have to make the best of your housemates."

"There's nothing good to be made of those two." Barbara turned back to Billy and Linda. "Those fuckers haven't helped us a bit."

Billy looked around the room. "You did all this work yourselves?"

"Yeah. All of it."

Suddenly, Todd seemed almost tongue-tied. "I just want to, uh, say thanks to the both of you, you know, for doing what you did."

"It's no problem, man," said Billy.

"But it is for me. Especially after the things I said—the way I threatened you." He hung his head slightly. "It's just that I saw what you were wearing, Linda, and it triggered something in me."

"It's fine, really. Billy and I thought you guys were assholes, too."

Barbara knew it was juvenile, but what she planned to say just felt cathartic. "Well, you were right about two of—"

"*Barbara!*"

"Okay, Todd. Okay."

"The way you saw me act isn't something I like others to see," he continued. "I'm not proud of it, and I just need you to forgive me."

"We forgive you," Billy said.

"But do you think that woman will ever be okay with us?" Linda asked.

"Probably not, but let's plow past the bad shit." Todd reached into his pocket. "Let's get stoned." He handed the pipe to Barbara after he'd filled it.

She took a substantial hit. Billy was closest to her, on the left hand side, so she turned to him, but he didn't move. A few seconds passed; his helmet bobbed up and down. "Okay, yeah," he said. "Sure."

"Billy!" Linda shouted. "You know you're not supposed to smoke that!"

His voice seemed jagged all the sudden. "But there's no team anymore." His hands became fists. "God, I loved that team! I knew some of those guys since I was a kid!"

The fists unclenched. "Now they're gone…"

Barbara re-extended the pipe. "Don't think about that stuff now."

"I'll try not to," Billy said. He took the pipe and brought it up to his mouth without removing his helmet. He had trouble getting the lighter to the green, but soon found a way to maneuver his fingers and Barbara's lighter between the chin guard and visor. When he exhaled, smoke curled up through all the holes in his helmet, around his mouth, ears and neck, even the top of his head.

"Man, it would be easier if you took off the helmet," said Todd.

Billy sounded uncertain again. "I, uh, have to keep it on."

"Why?"

"Because I'm not used to people seeing me scared, and, well, I don't want them seeing me that way."

"I don't think it's weird," Linda said. "You know I've always loved you in the helmet."

He nodded, seemed a bit embarrassed.

"Nobody's going to make you take it off," Barbara said. A part of her wished she had a helmet, too—somewhere her face could hide when things went wrong.

Billy realized he'd been bogarting the pipe. He offered it to Linda.

"Might as well, " she said. Taking the pipe, she drew in a small hit and coughed it back out.

"So," Barbara asked as snaky tendrils began to creep up her spine. "How long have you guys been together?"

"Since"—Linda coughed again—"freshman year"— and then again—"high school."

"Long time," said Todd.

"We'd like to get married," Billy added. "We just don't know when."

Linda's face fell. Billy sensed something was wrong, glanced over at her and stuttered helplessly when he realized the implications of what he'd said.

"It looks bad," Todd told her. "But maybe things won't be this way forever, and you two can get married when the time's right."

Linda smiled, but it looked thin. "I'm just so glad we found you. Billy is, too. I don't know how long we've been in that clock, alone. All day, I guess."

"I've been here since about 2:30," Barbara said.

"Did you come on foot?" Todd asked. "Didn't see your car."

Billy regained his voice. "We had a ride back home from the game, but the guy became an asshole. All Linda and I could do was run."

The pipe returned to Todd. He knocked out the ash and placed the pipe—along with his cigarettes after he tapped two out for himself and Barbara—on the end table beside him.

"Do you—do you mind if I have another hit?" Billy asked sheepishly. "It's just been so long and I—"

"Sure." Todd repacked the bowl. "And now that I think about it, I'm up for another round." He set the two cigarettes down. "Anyone else?"

Everyone was in, so Todd presented the bowl to Billy to start the round; Barbara gave him her lighter. "Thanks, guys," Billy said.

CHAPTER THIRTY-ONE

"I'm stoned as fuck!" Billy announced.

Todd nearly cackled. "I'm stoned as fuck, too!"

Barbara said nothing, but giggled a bit.

"Those assholes are assholes!" Linda shouted. "I don't know why we're even worried!"

"Yeah, fuck 'em!" Billy agreed. "I should go out there now, show them a thing or—"

At that moment, everyone heard descending footsteps on the stairs that led to the front of the room.

Billy coiled up on the couch. His confidence had evaporated in an instant. "What the fuck was that?" he shrieked.

Then a male voice—high-pitched and prissy—said, "Oh my, oh my, look how smart I am! I've found the *secret* way in!"

Barbara's giddy buzz fell dead. She looked over at Todd.

"I knew the upstairs was no good," he said. Then, "Where's your pole, Barbara?"

She knew where it was: still in the bathroom by the toilet.

"Shit, Barbara! Shit! How many times have I told you to keep up with it?"

"I'm sorry, Todd. I tried." But she really wasn't sorry, and she really hadn't tried. As angry and violent as she'd been for most of her life, she just couldn't stake an ass and hope to do it right. Her brain couldn't process the thought, and her conscience wouldn't allow it.

Todd looked around. He slammed his fists against his lap. "Damn it! I don't have mine, either!"

Linda trembled, wrapped herself around Billy. There

117

was no space between them now.

"You sit back," Todd said. "In fact, all of you sit back."
He arose.

Barbara wanted to pull Todd closer to her, for him to
say he wasn't leaving at all. Linda asked, "Where are you
going?"

"I've got to board the upstairs before anymore wander
down!" He stopped just as the asshole—a tall, thin blonde-
haired man, dressed in bondage gear—reached the bottom
of the staircase. He carried a whip. Todd didn't stare long.
He bent down, picked up an armload of stray wood, some
nails and a hammer.

"But, Todd!" Linda shrieked. "What do *we* do?"

"I don't think this guy is major-league. You're going to
have to…entertain him until I get some work done on that
doorway. No matter what he says or does, just stay nice."

"But can't you—" Billy began.

Todd seemed to know what the football player was
going to ask. "And risk a hundred more pouring down
those steps?" He spread his gaze across everyone on the
couch. "Right now, all I can do is wish you luck." Turning
away, he walked quickly—but not too quickly—past the
asshole, who regarded Todd's backside.

"Decent," he said. "But not my type."

Todd started up the stairs. To Barbara, it sounded like
two sets of feet were on them. One set going up. One set
going down.

Both sets stopped. "Would you like to see my—?"
started an elderly female voice.

"I'll certainly take a look when I'm finished," Todd said
without inflection. "Thanks for asking."

"That's fine, young man. I'll just wait for you
downstairs."

Footsteps resumed.

CHAPTER THIRTY-TWO

"What are you looking at?" asked the male asshole. He stood by the couch now, hands on his hips. The query seemed directed at both Barbara and Linda.

They said nothing.

He struck his whip against the floor. "Are you deaf? What are you looking at?"

Say something; say anything! Barbara's mind screamed, but Linda spoke first.

"Nothing, sir. We're just sitting here."

"Well, I know you're looking, so stop it! I'm not interested in bitches!" He gazed over at Billy, where his attention lingered. "I'm into the football hero, here. He's a breath of fresh air in a room full of hags!"

The asshole turned slightly. Barbara noted his chaps were ass-less.

The second asshole—an ancient woman in equally ancient-looking black, lacy dress and shawl—reached the bottom of the stairs, but didn't go directly to the couch. Instead, she looked around at the knickknacks first, seemed enchanted by them.

"But that's an old woman!" whispered Linda to Barbara.

"Anyone can be—"

"Bitches! Hush!" snapped the asshole in the ass-less chaps. "I have no interest in you!" He walked up to Billy, rubbed the top of his helmet. "Tall boy, I see," he said. "Six feet-four? Five?"

"Six," Billy said. "Six feet-six"

"Strong boy, too." He squeezed Billy's bicep; Billy flinched. "What'cha bench?"

"Uh, 350. Sometimes 375."

"Really? I would have thought 425, 450." He paused, seemed to sulk. "Whatever, you'll do."

Billy stuttered a bit. "Do for what?"

"No questions! Stand up!"

Linda grabbed Billy. "No!" she pleaded. "Don't do it!"

"Do you want him to become an asshole?" Barbara said to her.

"Of course not!"

"Then he has to do it!"

Billy looked at Linda. She nodded; he stood. Upstairs, the sound of hammering commenced.

"Now walk away from these bitches," said the asshole. "Stand in the middle of the room where I can see you better."

Billy and the asshole stopped halfway between the couch and the old asshole, who still cooed at the knickknacks, picking them up, studying them and dropping a few, but only if they were made of glass.

"Looks good. Real good." The asshole circled Billy. "So, what's your name?"

"B-Billy."

"Well, hello B-Billy. My name is None-of-Your-Fucking-Business." He titled his head. "I take it that's your girlfriend back there?"

"Y—yeah. Her name is…it's Linda."

The asshole sneered. "I don't care what her name is! I'm going to make you do things you don't want to do, right in front of her!" He cracked his whip again. "Bend over for me, Football Hero."

"You gotta do it!" Linda called from across the room. "You just gotta!"

"Well, you don't *just gotta*," the asshole said. "You could get all flustered and smack me around a bit. A big sexy jock such as yourself would love to do that to me, right?"

Billy said nothing. He bent over.

"Ah, looks like I had you pegged all wrong! I just *love* big, buff compliant boys that little old me can beat up and boss around!" The asshole walked behind Billy, studied his butt. "Nice, but bloody, bloody, bloody! Did that strapping black guy try to ass-ram you?"

"No," Billy said. "It was, uh, it was Barbara."

He smiled a vulpine smile. "There's been a lot of ass-ramming today, hasn't there? Seems everybody's had fun but little 'ole me. Isn't that sad?"

"Yes," Billy said. "It's very sad."

"Well, I won't be happy unless I get to mount you and ride you all across this room!" The asshole yanked Billy's pants down to his knees. "Take them the rest of the way off," he demanded.

"But—"

"*Do it!*"

Billy turned back to the couch. His helmet half-hid the expression on his face, but it still broke Barbara's heart, made her turn away. "Will you still love me, Linda?" he choked.

"You know I will!"

"*Très romantique,*" said the asshole as Billy kicked away his pants. Then the asshole mounted him, much like a rider would a steed. He swatted Billy's wounded ass with his whip and said, "Make like a bull, football hero!"

And so Billy bucked and bronked in his briefs, sometimes landing on and destroying the few pieces of wooden furniture Todd hadn't utilized for parts. He winced each time the asshole's whip lashed him.

On the other side of the room, the old asshole dropped the vase she'd been looking at and walked towards the sofa, turning first to Billy and the other asshole.

"No roughhousing indoors!" she admonished.

"Whatever, you old biddy," the asshole said as he dug his heels into Billy's sides. Barbara saw then that he wore spurs.

"No tea for you," retorted the old asshole. Then she sat down in the now vacant sofa across from Barbara and Linda. "I'm sorry for staying back there, but the décor was so charming, and I didn't want to interrupt that other man while he was chatting with your friend." She looked over at the asshole riding Billy and frowned. "Though I wouldn't have extended the courtesy if I'd known he'd be so rude."

Barbara just smiled, nodded. Maybe this asshole was barely an asshole at all, and poor Billy would suffer the brunt of the torture until Todd returned.

"That black man was in such a hurry," the old asshole continued. "Didn't have time to talk with me, but I understand. The world is so much faster now, and besides I—"

She hadn't stopped, but the sounds of Billy forced to play bronco made it difficult to hear her delicate, warbling voice. "What was that last thing you said?" Barbara asked.

"I said, I don't care much for black people. We're all white here, right? We can say that."

Barbara continued to smile.

"Say you don't care much for black people, dear. Make an old woman happy."

Linda nudged her. "Just do it."

"I—I don't care much for black people." Barbara wanted to wilt.

The old asshole began pouring tea from a porcelain kettle into a matching cup. Barbara stared. From whence these things had come, she had no clue.

The old asshole stopped pouring. "Oh, but where are my manners? Would you like some tea, too?"

"No, I—"

Barbara elbowed Linda and spoke beneath her breath. "We must."

"I said *no* politely, didn't I?" Linda whispered.

122

"But she's one of them; just say yes."

"What?" the old asshole screeched. "You kids gotta speak up!" She rammed a black horn into her left ear. "I'm a little hard of hearing!"

"Yes," Barbara said. "We'll both take some tea. Gladly."

"Such a well-spoken young lady! I'm impressed, seeing that most women these days are tramps and whores."

"Yes," said Barbara. "They're total tramps."

"Total whores," Linda agreed.

More cups were suddenly on the end table by her seat. The old asshole put down the ear horn, filled the cups and handed them to Barbara and Linda.

Barbara looked down at her tea.

"Come on. Have a sip. It's good for you."

She obeyed, expecting the taste of gas, or turpentine, or raw sewage. Instead, the tea had a light, pleasant flavor. Probably chamomile.

"Like the tea, dear?"

Barbara didn't hear her. The male asshole had requested that Billy make bull-sounds, and Billy had complied. "What did you say?" Barbara almost shouted.

"Use the ear horn, like I do!"

Barbara glanced down and saw a horn in her lap. She brought it to her ear and understood the woman as she repeated herself about the tea, even as the other asshole chastised Billy for his inability to sound convincingly like a bull.

"Yes," she said. "The tea is quite good. Thank you."

"Wonderful. So, are we all settled?"

"I guess so," Barbara said.

"Then let me tell you *all* about my children. She reached for her billfold. It spilled open as she extracted it from a massive pocket in her dress; a line of wallet-sized photos in plastic unfurled, and kept unfurling. Barbara feared it might be endless.

"There's Zephanarias and then Malakuk. They're both

in their sixties now. No wait, Malakuk is dead. He died when he was five." She lifted the wallet to face level. "Isn't my dead child beautiful?"

"Yes," Barbara nodded, and Linda nodded, too. "He's a good looking boy."

"But Zephanarias, he's still alive. He performs abortions now, somewhere up in Washington, maybe. I don't know, I've never been." She flipped a page. It was hard not to notice that every picture she turned to was the same black and white photograph of the same boy, perhaps age eight.

In the next room, something made a creaking sound. A few seconds later, Ellen peeked her head past the door facing, but, upon seeing the current situation, retracted it just as quickly.

Damn you! Barbara thought. *Come out here and take it with the rest of us!*

The old asshole turned another plastic flap. "That's Jebizekial." And more flaps and more flaps. "And there's Habaniah, Jobiah and Elijahu." Same damn kid.

"I bet they grew up to be handsome men," Linda said before taking an apprehensive sip of tea.

The asshole scowled at Linda. "No! They were useless, good-for-nothing boys who got what they deserved!" Her hands shook; she seemed suddenly agitated. "You nice young ladies should really stop looking at me like that."

"We're not looking at you in any way," Barbara said, and quickly thought to add, "my dear lady."

"You are! You're staring at me and accusing me!" She threw down her tea. "But I didn't kill my only child, Kyle, bury him in the dirt floor of the basement and construct an elaborate fantasy world! No, I did not!"

"We never said you did!"

Her eyes reddened. "But you *implied* it!"

Just behind them, the whip lashings and bull sounds stopped. "Foreplay's over," the male asshole announced.

"Now drop those briefs, Billy Boy! Spread—"

At that moment, a wet and meaty rip erased his words. The old bitch hadn't heard, but Barbara had, and knew what it meant. She wanted to close her eyes so she wouldn't see, but that might alert the asshole. Barbara just wished there was a way to warn Linda.

"And I'm not crazy!" The old asshole shrieked, flailing her arms. "Why do you people always—" Abruptly, she reared back her head. A blood geyser erupted as Todd's pole shot from her mouth and kept going, ultimately protruding half a foot above her lips.

Linda screamed and scrambled backwards over the couch. She bolted straight into the wall. Sobbing, she slid down it.

Barbara turned and saw the football player, still in his underwear, standing over the dead male asshole. He looked defenseless.

"Sorry guys," Todd said, wrenching his pole from both the asshole and the back of the couch. "If you survive long enough, you could see this hundreds if not thousands of times, so try to get used to it." Then he picked up the male asshole, dropped him onto the couch with the old one. Getting behind the sofa, he pushed it towards the room with the clock.

Barbara looked back at Linda and then again at Billy. Both seemed nearly catatonic now. She didn't know what to say or do to fix that.

When Todd reemerged from the room, he walked over to Billy and put a hand on his shoulder. "You're a strong guy," he said. "You can take this."

Billy's voice was reedy, almost inaudible. "I've—I've never—never seen anyone die—die before. Especially not—not like—like that."

"It's not a person, Billy. It's an asshole." Todd guided

him to the couch; Billy moved like something only pretending to be alive. "Come on, sit down. Let's get your pants back on."

Barbara went to Linda as Todd tended to her boyfriend. She said nothing, just shook like the Chihuahua her mom used to own, and Barbara cursed her brain for making her think of her mother again. "Let me help you up," she said to Linda.

"No! Let me stay!"

"But Billy's on the couch now. He's okay, and he wants to see you."

"Billy?" she said. "Billy's on the couch?"

"I'll take you to him." Barbara lifted her, and she flopped like a rag doll when Barbara put her on the couch by Billy just as Todd helped him pull up his pants. Billy looked at her, seemed like he wanted to say something, maybe hold her, but he could do neither. Barbara took a seat on the opposite side of the couch.

Todd remained standing. "It's the way it is," he said.

He had a point, Barbara knew. But—god, did those poor kids have to see that? It was asshole death, but death like human death that would otherwise be tantamount to murder. It was bad, she realized, when the only defense she had was an act that would make her a monster.

"Talk with them a little more, Barbara," Todd said. "I have to get back up there and finish."

Barbara spent the next ten minutes sitting close to Billy as he sat close to Linda. Linda had barely said a word—in fact, she leaned her head on the armrest, mouth slightly ajar and eyes pointed up at the ceiling. Billy, however, had started talking, sometimes spewing out so many words Barbara just had to sit back and listen.

"That could have been me back in the clock," he said, looking down at the rug. "Me with a pole up my ass and out my mouth, just like that ma—like that asshole."

"It could have been, but it wasn't," Barbara said. "And it's just like Todd told you. That asshole wasn't human. It wasn't even an animal."

"But he looked human! And she looked human! And, oh god…"

"There was no love in them. You know that guy was going to rape you, right?"

"Yeah, I know." He looked up at Barbara. His eyes were dull and watery. "But maybe that would have been better."

"No." She hugged him close; it amazed her, how much genuine tenderness she could feel towards someone she'd only known for a few hours. "It wouldn't be better."

"I guess—I guess I've got to be a man. Got to live with it like Todd said. But I don't want to. I just—"

"Is that woman gone?" Linda said suddenly, her voice floating up to them like a ghost. Barbara broke her embrace with Billy so he could embrace her.

"She's gone," Billy said. "She's gone, and maybe she was never here."

"Never here?"

"Yeah, never here."

"But she was, Billy. I remember her. I remember—"

"Shhh. Try to forget."

Linda leaned into him, so he stroked her hair, gave her a kiss. "It'll be okay," he continued. "Just sit here for a while. Sit with me. Try to forget."

She closed her eyes then. He closed his, too.

Barbara got up. It felt like too personal a moment for her to remain sitting there.

CHAPTER THIRTY-THREE

At the bottom of the stairwell, Barbara looked up at Todd, who still worked on sealing the entranceway. "Need any help?" she called.

"No," he said. "I'm about done here."

She was glad he'd said that. It felt like she needed more downtime. Turning from Todd, she looked at the boarded windows and door. Made the place seem like it had no way in or out. There were small gaps between the planks, of course, and she considered peering through one, just to remember there was something out there, a world. Instead, she went back towards the room with the clock. She opened the door, entered and closed the door again. She didn't want it ajar if Billy or Linda were to get up and walk by.

It seemed Todd had found a sheet and draped it over the sofa on which the two bodies lay. This made it easy to pretend it was just an old, disused piece of furniture awaiting the trash heap. Still, a part of her wanted to throw back the sheet and scoot the sofa right in front of the clock. Ellen and Harold would have no choice but see it when they emerged. Maybe they'd wake up then, wake up and realize they had to pull their own weight in this house, and that stakes were too high to indulge in pettiness.

Barbara quashed that thought. Maybe it was too extreme. Rather than make a showcase of corpses, she went to the TV set, considered picking it up and bashing it. She'd bashed old TVs before. Cathode ray tubes always produced a satisfying *pop*. But then she thought again of Billy and Linda. They'd surely hear and, not knowing what had happened, be terrified.

She bent down. Turned the set on. She remembered it

was channel 31 on which the newscaster had appeared, so she went there, expecting to find more static.

What she found instead was a crystal-clear black and white picture, filled by the newscaster she'd barely glimpsed and heard earlier. Now she could see he was a thin, dark headed man who wore horn-rimmed glasses.

She opened her mouth to call for Todd and Billy and Linda, but closed it quickly. She couldn't let those kids come into this room. She had to bring the TV to them.

But that meant unplugging it. Barbara feared the picture might go away—replaced forever with static—if she were to do that. She considered her limited options before deciding to accept the risk.

She unplugged the set, began pushing it out of the room just as Todd stopped nailing and called down from the stairs.

"What are you doing down there?" he asked.

"The TV works! There's a news show on, and I'm taking the set into the living room!"

"My god! You'd better get those two out of the clock when you're done. They might want to see."

Barbara stopped pushing. "Can't they just stay there?"

"Come on, Barbara. All you have to do is knock. You don't have to go in."

Grimacing, she rapped her knuckles on the door.

"What!" Ellen shouted. Her voice seemed more than a little distant.

"I've found a TV station that works. They're talking about what's happening outside."

First the first time, the woman sounded more surprised than pissed. "Really?"

"Yeah, really, so you should get your ass out here because I'm sure the clock doesn't have a TV."

"No, Harold! You stay!" Barbara heard Ellen bark. "I'll

tell you what's going on when I get back!"

Barbara and Todd took a seat by Billy and Linda. Ellen stood well behind them. Suddenly: the sound of approaching footsteps. Everyone turned, but it was only Harold.

"I told you to stay in that clock!" Ellen shouted. "Your daughter needs you!"

"But I wanted to find out what's going on!" He looked over at Linda, waved to her, but she never turned around to see him.

On screen, the newscaster said, "More reports are coming in by the minute, uh…second. I don't know if I can keep up with this…flood. But I'll try for you, all my untransformed brothers and sisters out there, hanging on my words, trying to stay safe in a world of flux.

"It seems that regular people are becoming… What's this? No, that can't be right. Are becoming…*assholes*, and by assholes, I don't mean the butt-part. I mean total dicks that cannot be killed. Ladies and gentlemen, I apologize for using such language on air, but, really, it's the only way to adequately express the nature of this ongoing crisis."

"Can't be killed?" Todd said. "Shit, if I could, I'd call the station and tell them how it's done."

Ellen shushed him.

"Still," the newscaster continued, "I'd like to stress that none of this is confirmed at the moment." He placed a finger against his earpiece. "Okay, it's all confirmed, and— hold on, ladies and gentlemen. Seems we're about to hear a brief report from Dr. Tim, our resident science expert."

The scene changed. An elderly guy in a lab coat sat behind a huge oak desk. Long, skeletal fingers tapped at the wood. Anatomical charts of reproductive organs hung over his head as he spoke, his voice a monotone. "It is estimated that by the end of tomorrow 83.4% of the Earth's population will be assholes. Prior to today, only

38.5% were assholes."

The voice of the newscaster, off screen: "My God, Dr. Tim! That's an astronomical increase!"

"Indeed it is. And in two days, if things progress as they are progressing now, it is estimated that the Earth's population will, for the most part, consist entirely of assholes."

"Well, that's fucking depressing!" Ellen said.

Todd took the opportunity to shush her.

The scene switched from Dr. Tim to the newscaster. He took his glasses off and wiped them, then wiped his eyes. "Ladies and gentlemen, law and order is a thing of the past. Soon, the only non-assholes will probably be survivor nuts, holed underground. Perhaps we should have all been survivor nuts, because the human race is—" The newsman's dour expression suddenly brightened; he pressed a finger back to his earpiece. "Wait, there might still be hope! I am now receiving word as to what you— all the brave non-assholes watching this broadcast—can do. Do not stay indoors. *I repeat, do not stay indoors.* Go immediately to the nearest of these shelters." A scroll of place names started at the bottom of the screen. "Here you will find safety. Here you can escape the untold madness that grips our world today."

Text that read *Anders Middle School* traveled across the set.

"That's my old school!" Billy exclaimed. "It's only about a mile from here!"

Linda looked alive for the first time since the old asshole's death. "We've got to go there, Billy!" She clutched at him. "Right now!"

"But baby, we don't have a car."

"I have a truck," Todd said. "They've busted out her headlights, flattened her tires, but she could probably go a mile."

Linda turned to him, clasped her hands. "Will you

take us, Todd?"

"Let's think a little before we act, okay."

"What's to think about?" Her eyes were wide, almost wild. "That man on TV told us to go!"

"It just doesn't sound like the best idea. It's only a mile, sure, but think about the roads."

"They were crazy nine hours ago," Barbara said.

"But he wouldn't have told us to leave if they hadn't gotten better!"

"Maybe," Todd said, "but we're protected here; the boards have held. I can't say how long that'll stay true, but I know out there, for a mile, there's nothing but *them*. No walls to shield us."

She turned back to Billy. "Convince them we have to go! We'll be safer, a lot safer, and other people will be there—maybe doctors and scientists, too!"

"Scientists at the middle school?" Barbara asked incredulously.

"It doesn't matter! I don't feel safe here anymore!" She pulled away when Billy reached out to her. "I can take those assholes for a mile. Really, I can."

"You sure?" he asked.

"I just want out of this house."

Billy looked over at Todd. "She wants to go," he said, "and maybe it'd be good to be around more people."

Todd said nothing, seemed to think.

"If you can take us, Todd, I'd find some way to repay you."

Todd tapped his fingers on his knees, exhaled. "I still don't much like the idea," he said, finally. "But if we do this, we should do it as a team."

"Hell no!" said Ellen. "I've got the clock, and there's no way I'm taking my daughter outside. Harold and I are—"

"But—" Harold began.

Ellen stared him down. "Harold and I are staying, and that's that!"

132

"Whatever." Todd addressed Barbara then. "You can either stay here with them or come with us."

She turned, regarded Ellen and Harold. The choice was clear. "I'll come with you," she said.

Todd stood, walked over to Ellen. "Lock the door behind us, but don't start re-boarding it until you see that we're gone. Something could go wrong out there."

"Well, I don't think we should risk—"

"Don't board the door until you see that we're gone!"

"Fine! You don't have to yell, you bastard!"

Todd stepped away from her and made the first move towards the door.

CHAPTER THIRTY-FOUR

Eight minutes later, the boards were off, but the door remained locked. Barbara, Todd, Billy and Linda stood by it. Todd and Barbara carried their poles, and so did Billy, one that Todd had fashioned for him from a wooden curtain rod, broken in half. Ellen stood farther from them, but was ready to slam the door at a moment's notice. Harold was nowhere to be seen.

"I'll go first," Todd said. "Billy, you follow me. Barbara, take up the rear so Linda doesn't have to."

Barbara got into place. Billy's broad shoulders blocked Todd from her view. She knew Billy was big, but it hadn't dawned on her until then just how big he was. It'd be great if he could use his football skills and just barrel outside, block assholes and tackle them to the ground. Of course, that would only work if he planned to become an asshole himself.

Barbara heard the door start to open. The line surged forward, and she moved with it. The door slammed shut behind her.

There were at least a hundred of them—men, women and children. Rather than being clustered mindlessly around the periphery of the house, assholes were strewn about the yard, some relaxing on the grass or in hammocks, others ordering junk food from a big colorful tent as still more waited in line for three carnival-style rides that had been set up near the property's end.

"Shit!" said someone holding a candied apple. "There they are!"

All eyes turned. Assholes dropped what they were doing—even jumped from seats in moving rides—and started towards the four of them.

The truck was less than ten feet from the porch. Todd, Barbara and Billy hurried to it and got inside. Linda plopped down hard on her boyfriend's lap. Sandwiched between the other three, Barbara tried to imagine she was encased in a warm cocoon.

Todd rammed his keys into the ignition. The engine started; he put it in gear. Everyone bounced as the truck ran on its rims over rocky and uneven ground. "Sorry, Old Betsy," Todd said beneath his breath.

Suddenly, an asshole ran out in front of them. Todd swerved, but almost immediately a second ran out, and then a third and a fourth and a fifth—more and more until it seemed assholes were spinning around the truck in an unbroken ring. Todd slammed on his breaks.

"Just go!" the cheerleader begged. "Please!"

"I can't! If I hit one, I become an asshole!"

Through their touching legs, Barbara felt Billy start to tremble. "What do we do now, Todd?" he asked.

Todd said nothing. Nobody said anything. Assholes amassed all around the sides of the truck, atop its hood and inside its bed. To Barbara, it looked as though the world had become nothing but faces.

A morbidly obese asshole used his girth to knock down and squeeze past those in front of him. He reached the window on Linda and Billy's side and leaned against it.

"Hi," he said, breathing heavily.

"Hello," said everyone in the truck.

He raised his left hand. In it, he held a massive hotdog—at least two feet in length. "I've already had five of these big boys," he said, "and I really don't think I can down another." He faced Linda. "Would you like a bite, young lady?" he asked her, smiling. "You'll like it."

Her voice trembled. "No, thank you."

His smile vanished. "Wrong answer!" The asshole grabbed Linda by the hair and yanked her head back.

When she opened her mouth to scream, he shoved the hotdog down her throat—and kept shoving.

"Oh god, no!" Billy shouted as Todd leaned over Barbara and tried to perform an awkward Heimlich maneuver on Linda. Barbara pressed herself deep into the seat so Todd might have more room, but the hotdog was down at least a foot, and the cheerleader was turning blue.

"Let me try!" Billy forced the door open. With Linda in his arms, he exited the compartment. Assholes pulled away from the truck and began forming a circle around them. Some laughed. Others pointed or snapped pictures.

For almost a minute, Linda shook in Billy's arms and turned bluer and bluer as he tried everything in his power to dislodge the hotdog. When she shook no more, Billy continued performing the Heimlich maneuver; assholes continued to point and laugh.

"She's gone, Billy," Todd said.

"No, she's not!" Beyond his helmet, his face was scarlet. "She's not gone! I can save her!"

"Just get back in the—"

"Looks like you need a new girlfriend," interjected a grinning asshole.

Billy shook with rage.

"Really," he continued. "She's total maggot food."

Billy released Linda, and she fell on her face, one arm underneath her chest, the other flung to her side. "Fuck you, motherfucker!" he screamed.

"No, Billy!" Todd shouted. "Use the pole!"

Barbara put her face in her hands as Billy launched his bulk at the asshole, knocked him off his feet and pinned him to the ground. The host of assholes clustered tighter around them, cheering Billy on as he pounded the asshole's face with both fists.

"Yeah, beat his bitch ass!" one shouted.

Billy began to scream; Todd slammed his foot on the gas.

"But Billy—" Barbara started.

"He's an asshole now. We've got to go."

Todd was right. With the assholes distracted, the path to the road was unobstructed. Barbara looked out the rear window. Assholes still gave chase—some throwing rocks, others eggs. Though they couldn't keep up, they never slowed down.

"Don't look back," Todd said. "Forget that place exists."

Barbara turned towards the front. No assholes, and the road couldn't be more than fifty feet away. For the first time, she felt she might actually see the inside of a shelter.

But, near the boundary with the road, two lines of assholes emerged from the surrounding woods, one coming from the west, the other from the east. They met in the middle and formed a single line that spanned the property. Assholes in it adjusted position quickly until one stood three feet from the other. Again, Todd stopped the truck.

"Now what!" Barbara shouted. Behind them, the other assholes kept running.

Todd thought for only a second. "A game of chicken," he said.

She couldn't have heard him right. "What?" she asked.

He tapped the gas. "You heard me."

"But that's crazy, Todd!"

"Is it?" he said, slowly gaining speed.

"Yes, it is! They won't move because they won't die!"

"I was planning on hitting them."

Had Todd gone insane? "What!" she shouted. "You can't—"

"I'll hit those assholes. Then I'll jump out and stake them. If I do it fast enough, maybe I won't transform."

"No," Barbara said. "Don't risk—"

"Do you have a better idea?"

She was silent.

He put a hand on her knee. "If it doesn't work, I want

you to stake me."

"But Todd—"

He withdrew the hand, clenched it. "*Stake me!*"

"Okay, Todd! Okay!"

"Good, Barbara. That's what I wanted to hear." He slammed his foot down hard on the gas pedal.

The force generated pushed Barbara back in her seat. "Slow down!" she yelled.

"No! Can't let those assholes know I'm scared!"

"Todd, I'm in here, too!" But he showed no signs of relenting. Barbara reached for the seatbelt and pulled, but it was stuck.

Just then, she had a scary thought. What if she became an asshole vicariously, by virtue of being with a man who plowed over assholes with his truck? That would mean she'd go away, maybe die. She didn't feel ready for either of those things.

The line was close now. Asshole in it didn't budge, didn't even blink.

Then the engine began to sputter. Todd looked down at the instrument panel before turning to his left. Through the window, he saw the bag of sugar that had been rammed into the gas tank.

Barbara recoiled as Todd slammed his fists against the steering wheel. He continued to strike it as the truck slowed to a crawl and came to a dead stop. Assholes from the line stood a matter of feet away.

The road taunted Barbara with its closeness. The line of assholes began to break. Hope dried up in her and blew away.

Todd seized Barbara with the hand that wasn't holding the pole. "We've got to go back," he said.

"No, Todd!" She yanked her hand free, pulled her body inside the truck. Assholes from the line had reached the hood. "I don't want to!"

He turned. His face was scrunched and troll-like again.

"We don't have time for this shit!" he shouted.

"I can't do it! We were so—"

"Would you rather run a mile with them chasing you?"

"No, but—"

"And god knows how many are out on the streets!" He grabbed her hand and yanked her from the truck. At that moment, the closest asshole unleashed a loud, sewer-scented belch mere inches from her face. Barbara could almost see the green gas cloud. Her stomach rolled. She wanted to gag. Clutching her wrist, Todd turned from the asshole and ran. "Come on!" he shouted to her. "Move!"

Barbara found it odd, running toward things from which she'd just ran. She tried not to think of the assholes behind her, to tune them out of existence.

Todd and Barbara veered left. The assholes veered left. When they veered right, the assholes did likewise. The wall of running bodies drew ever closer until it filled Barbara's vision. There couldn't be more than twenty feet between them now, and she could feel the breath of those behind her. To become the meat of an asshole sandwich seemed like destiny.

An egg splattered against her face. Barbara barely felt it. Something harder grazed her cheek. Might have been a rock, but she had no way of knowing.

The twain met. To Barbara, it felt like hitting water from a very tall diving board. She had to close her eyes and let Todd lead her. It seemed safer there, in the dark, but it didn't feel like they were going anywhere, just being swept like broken seaweed across an ocean of assholes. "Excuse me," she said as they bumped and scraped up against her. She felt hands in all of her pockets; her wallet was surely gone.

Then the voices started:

"God, you're fat!"

"Want some fried chicken, Blackie?"

"Hey baby, wanna mercy-fuck?"

Assholes continued to join the choir until their words meshed together in a torrent of sound indistinguishable from a roar.

Barbara wanted to swoon. She smelled their body odor, sometimes their urine and feces. She tried breathing out her mouth. "I'm so sorry for bothering you," she said. "Pardon me, please. I'm sorry for not looking at you. I'm sorry for not taking what you offer. Oh god, pardon me!"

Suddenly, Todd's hand disappeared. She heard a meaty rip and the sound of him screaming, "Yeah, I know how it's done, so get back—please and thank you!"

She opened her eyes. Todd had speared a middle-aged businessman asshole, complete with briefcase. The other assholes saw this and pulled back just enough for Todd and Barbara to plow past them.

But the path wasn't clear. Just ahead, a tattooed asshole held up a pamphlet titled THE MASTER RACE. "Did you know—" he started

"No, I didn't, but thank you," Todd said as he rushed by him.

"Hey, let's take a picture together!" said a greasy asshole to Barbara.

"Sorry!" Barbara said without turning. "No time!"

The steps were just feet away. Barbara spun around. Assholes who'd witnessed Todd's prowess with the pole were starting to regroup. They stepped over their dead comrade, some holding out hands that clutched dildos or magazines or trays with samples or more hotdogs, others yammering still on cell phones.

Barbara froze. Todd grabbed her wrist again, pulled her up the steps and onto the porch. There, he turned the knob, but it was still locked. He beat his fists against the door. "Ellen! Harold! Let us in!"

Barbara listened, but heard nothing, not even approaching

footsteps from inside.

"Damn it! Let us in, right now!"

Harold's voice was frantic behind the door: "We have to do it!"

"We don't have to do anything," Ellen responded cool-ly.

"Yes!" Barbara shouted. "Yes, you do!" She felt a hand on her back.

"I really think you should take that picture with me," the asshole said. Smiling, he showed her his dirty, rotten teeth.

Todd kicked the door, rattled its frame. "Let us the fuck in!"

Within the house, there was the sound of sudden scrambling. The pamphleteer handed his MASTER RACE pamphlet to Todd. Barbara turned. The mass of assholes was fighting its way onto the porch.

The lock disengaged. Harold opened the door. Barbara and Todd spilled inside. An arm and a camera entered, too. The lens pointed at Barbara on the floor. A flash ignited.

Todd jumped up. "I'm sorry," he said as he tried to close the door behind the asshole and take care of other arms, now snaking through. "So sorry."

CHAPTER THIRTY-FIVE

Once the door was locked, Todd glared at Ellen and Harold, but didn't act on his apparent anger. He turned from them without uttering a word and started re-boarding the door. Assholes behind it pounded with their fists and kicked with their feet.

"Where are those kids?" Harold asked.

"Linda's dead," Barbara choked. "Billy's an asshole."

Harold looked forlorn, but Ellen's face didn't change. She said, "Sad, I guess, but the house was getting a little crowded."

Barbara wanted to run at Ellen, bring her to the floor and pound her like Billy had the asshole. She wanted to help Todd with the door so that impulse might fade. But she found herself able to do neither. Her knees were weak, so she sat on the floor between Todd and Helen. She felt tears start to pool in her eyes. Then the tears poured out, not only for Billy and Linda, but also for her mother and brother and sister and everyone else who'd died that day or become assholes. Barbara made no effort to staunch the flow.

"Thought you were a tough girl," Ellen said above her.

"Give it a rest," Todd growled. "She's seen more than you have."

Barbara didn't know how long she'd spent on the floor, sobbing, rocking back and forth before she felt a hand on her shoulder. She gasped, recoiled—but saw it was only Todd.

He bent down to help her, but Barbara stood on her own accord and followed him back to the sofa. They sat in front of the TV. It still showed the newscast.

Barbara barely paid attention. She was thinking of Linda's blue face, Billy's last scream.

"What the shit?" Todd said.

Barbara looked up from her thoughts. "What is it, Todd?"

"Weren't you watching?"

She shook her head. "Not really."

On screen, the newsman appeared more manic than ever. He was surrounded by Teleprompters—dozens of them—and assistants wheeled in more by the second.

"There are reports of this phenomena occurring in all the major cities of the United States," he said, "and even in such insignificant and disgusting towns as Pigfart, Nebraska, Phlegmsburg, Ohio and Dunghole, Tennessee." Additional place names were added to the scroll of text at the bottom of the screen, including *The Emerald Castle* and *Yo Mama's*. "Ladies and gentlemen," the newscaster continued, "please go immediately to the closest listed shelter. I repeat, *go to the closest listed shelter*. Absolutely no one is safe."

Barbara turned to Todd. "Yo Mama's?"

"Just keep watching," he said.

The newscaster glanced quickly at various Teleprompters, as if trying to decide which he should read from next. Finally, he chose one. "The President of the United States is an asshole! The King and Queen of England, and all members of Parliament and the House of Lords are assholes! The Pope is an asshole! Rip his picture up, fair viewers! Rip it up now!" He looked away from the Teleprompter then, face grave. "I could continue reading, but it's safe to say every world government and religious leader is, in fact, an asshole."

Someone shouted off-camera. The newscaster turned just in time to see a suit-clad, hairpiece-wearing man barreling down on him. This man pounced upon the anchor, and both went to the ground.

"I apologize for that unseemly display, ladies and gentlemen," the attacker said upon arising. "I only wish I could have put an earlier stop to his perniciousness. That man was offering misleading information and directing people to shelters that were, in fact, traps."

"He was, I'm sorry to report, an asshole, but rest assured I have the information you need and will relate it before he regains consciousness." He cleared his throat, fidgeted with his tie. "Sadly, this is the End of Days. It's time to panic. It's time to round up your children and put a bullet in each of their heads before putting a bullet in your own. This may sound harsh; this may sound unforgiving, but, my god, do you want your precious loved ones to become total fucking assholes? I, for one, do—"

At that moment, a great clamor, and another guy bounded into the studio and attacked the second guy just as he'd attacked the first.

"Don't listen to him, either," the third anchor said, as the first and second lay on the floor. "Do not go to the shelters listed below." To someone off-camera: "Could we get those to stop scrolling anytime soon?" Then, back to the viewing audience: "Do not kill your children or yourself. No. This is what you need to do: rage against these assholes. Push them. Punch them. Kill them. Whatever. Just stand up and—"

Another newscaster emerged, pummeled the third, took his spot, but lasted less than thirty seconds before a fifth pummeled *him*, and he lasted only a second or two, uttering just a single word when yet another body sent him crashing to the floor.

The tenth newscaster finally had a chance to speak. "Those guys were all assholes, but so am I!" The man cackled, and the nine other newsmen arose and started to dance, gyrating loathsomely, some losing their clothes. Dr. Tim soon joined them.

CHAPTER THIRTY-SIX

Barbara didn't turn off the TV, but threw a glass sculpture of a poodle at it, shattering the screen.

Ellen and Harold scrambled into the living room. "What was that?" Harold shouted.

"I busted the TV, okay!"

"What?" Ellen said. "Why did you—"

"Because it was full of assholes!" Barbara sank back into the cushion. "I just need a cigarette, right now."

"Me too," Todd said. He reached into a shirt pocket, frowned, and reached into another one. When they all turned up empty, he tried his pants. "Where are they? Wait, I know." He looked to the end table. They weren't there; his weed was gone, too.

He looked over at Barbara. "Did you get my smokes?"

She shook her head.

"Harold," Todd said. "You know where my smokes are, don't you."

"I—yes—but, uh—"

Todd got up, walked deliberately over to him. "Give them back," he demanded, hand outstretched.

"I can't."

Todd stared him down. "You can, and you will."

"But I, uh—threw them away."

"*Threw them away?* You don't *fuck* with another man's cigarettes!"

"But you were leaving, and you forgot them and—"

"You could have waited until we were gone! But you weren't even looking, were you? You were too busy tossing my shit!" His eyes narrowed to slits. "Did you throw away the weed, too?"

"No, I—I flushed it."

"*Flushed it?*"

"Well, it *is* illegal," Ellen interjected.

The shouting continued, but Barbara felt lost in her own world. No cigarettes. No weed. No. Impossible. It wouldn't have been so bad if they'd run out, but having both torn away so unexpectedly was too much. She felt the sudden need to rip off the boards and fling herself to the assholes. Life without smoke was madness.

She was up and on her feet before she knew it. She walked past a glowering Todd and a cringing Harold, went into the kitchen.

There was a trashcan in the corner by the door. Barbara knelt beside it and looked inside.

"God!" said Ellen, staring at her from the living room. "Are you that much of an addict?"

"Shut your fuckhole!" Barbara turned back to the trashcan. The cigarettes weren't just broken. They were shredded, impossible to smoke. But there had to be a way. She just needed to think.

Her eyes darted to a newspaper, likewise in the trash. She could remove that, yes. Remove it and wrap the tobacco grounds in it and smoke them.

Suddenly, Todd was behind her. "Stop," he said.

But she continued to dig. It made her feel a little crazy to think she might have already smoked the last cigarette of her life.

"Please, Barbara. Harold still had my pipe." He held it out in front of her. "I think I can scrape a bit of resin out of it."

She jumped up, trashcan in hand. "Why did it have to be Billy and Linda? Why? They wouldn't have done this to us! They weren't two complete *fuckers!*" She threw the can across the room, scattering refuse.

"Shhh." He unscrewed the pipe. "Let's scrape this thing and relax."

CHAPTER THIRTY-SEVEN

Harold took a seat by Barbara as Todd worked with the pipe, gathering resin in a sticky black ball on the end table. "I'm sorry," Harold said. "It might have been a bad thing to do, but I hate smoke and I really thought you were gone."

Barbara wanted to say *Well, I hate you*, but held her tongue.

"I'll tell you what. I'll let you smoke what Todd gets out of that pipe, and I won't complain a bit."

"Only because you know that's the last of it," she said.

"You don't need to apologize," said Ellen, re-entering the room. "Not to a couple of criminals."

Barbara made to rush Ellen, but Todd blocked her with his arm. "Do that," he said, "and she wins."

"You know, I used to smoke that stuff in high school," Ellen continued. "But I grew up."

Todd was right. It was tempting to lash out—to do all the things to Ellen she imagined doing, things that would no doubt prove blissfully cathartic—but she made herself view the intrusion as a test of her will, one she had to pass. She breathed in and out, exhaling anger as Harold continued to apologize.

"Really, if I could do it over again, I'd—" A look of concern fell over his face. He turned to Ellen. "Hear that?" he asked her.

"What? You falling all over yourself?"

"Just listen! It's a rumbling sound…"

She turned from him. "You're imagining things."

"No, Ellen, I'm—" Harold's eyes widened; he grabbed his junk. "Oh god! I feel it in my balls now!"

"What the hell?" Ellen looked as though she might slap him.

But Todd also appeared concerned. He stopped scraping the pipe. "I feel it too," he said to Harold.

Harold blanched.

"You're both crazy! You're both—" Ellen's mouth closed, then went slack.

"I told you!" Harold cried. "You hear it now! Maybe you even *feel* it!"

She nodded; her breasts jiggled slightly.

"Does this place have a generator?" Barbara asked.

"How should any of us know?" Ellen shot back.

Todd shook his head. "If there were one, we'd have already heard it." He paused, regarded his crotch. "And I don't believe a generator would cause this much vibration."

"My nuts are rattling, Todd!" Harold said, eyes darting, hands clawing at cushions.

"You think I can help that?"

"What could cause them to rattle? *What!*"

"God, you're pathetic!" Ellen shrieked.

"If it's not a generator," Barbara asked, an attempt to regain control of the conversation, "then what is it?"

Todd arose, motioned toward the nearest window. Barbara and Ellen followed. Harold attempted to do likewise.

"Stay back!" Ellen roared at him.

"But I want to see what's out there!" he pleaded.

"You probably won't be able to handle it!"

He sighed. Falling back, he became something like a sack on the couch.

CHAPTER THIRTY-EIGHT

At the window, everyone but Harold squinted through individual gaps between the boards.

"Oh my god!" said Barbara.

"Shit!" said Ellen.

"Motherfucker!" said Todd.

Harold bounded from his seat and made for the window. He pushed his wife out of the way. "It might be the government!" he said, looking out. "Or the National Guard!"

Ellen's forehead vein throbbed. "Are you blind? Does that look like the National fucking Guard to you?"

There were no government tags or insignias on a host of solid white, oversized passenger vans—molester vans—from the 70s. Everyone watched the phalanx move onto the property. It seemed endless.

"How many do you think there are?" Barbara asked Todd.

"I don't even want to count," he said.

The closest vans reached the floodlit area. Barbara saw long, metallic things tied atop them. It didn't take her long to realize they were ladders.

Just outside the window, individual assholes banded together and converged at the front, sides and back of the house, gathering in unbroken and unblinking rows. No more fake outs or trial runs. Then they began murmuring, louder and louder until their words were audible through the wall.

Barbara and Todd took steps back. Ellen slammed her hands against her ears, hummed.

Harold, however, was transfixed at the window. "That looks like a sledgehammer! Oh shit, that *is* a sledgehammer!"

"Yes, it's probably a sledgehammer," Todd said. "Just calm down."

"I can't! I can't calm down!"

"Get away from that window, Harold!" shrieked Ellen, hands still on her ears.

"No! I have to see what's going on!"

"Listen to your wife," Barbara said.

"But if I can see it, it's not so bad. I mean, it's still bad—but not knowing is worse, you know? Just waiting to... Shit!" He began to flail. "That's an axe! A fucking axe!"

Todd returned to the window, wrapped his arms around Harold's waist and wrenched him from the sill.

Harold hit Todd with fists loosely coiled. "Get your hands off me!"

"Ellen, I think I'm going to smack your husband," Todd said. "Full in the face."

She shrugged. "Why the hell should I mind?"

Todd turned back to Harold, slapped him. Harold went limp. Todd caught him before he collapsed, but even then he tried to sink. His left cheek was red. Tears welled in his eyes. He looked away from Todd. When Ellen scowled at him, he faced the wall.

"Look at me!" Todd shook him until he obeyed. "It's going to happen—they're going to get in—and, like it or not, we're going to deal with the situation!"

Harold just quaked.

"So start dealing with it!"

Todd released Harold. He fell to the floor just as the first arm breached the window to the left of the door. The second entered through the same window, lower left corner. The third slid between boards on the other side of the room.

Harold pissed himself, jumped up and took off running in the direction of the clock.

"Don't you *dare* go back there!" Todd seized his ass-ramming pole. "If you do, so help me..."

He slowed to a stop, looked back. "But—"

"But nothing! You're going to stay with the rest of us

and do your job! You too, Ellen!"

Grudgingly, Harold went with the others to spots where arms had entered.

Barbara swatted one of them, but didn't find much satisfaction in that. She began beating it, and Ellen soon joined her.

"Stop!" Todd shouted. "That might be enough to make you both assholes!"

"They're trying to break in!" Barbara said. "It's not assholish to stop them!"

"But it's not our house!"

"Well then, what the hell are we supposed to do?" Ellen snapped.

"Just get them out, as gently as possible!"

Boards failed. A sizable gap opened in Barbara's side of the window. Three arms snaked through, their hands clutching Barbara's shoulders, pulling her backwards.

"Sucks to be you," Ellen said seconds before arms plowed through the right side. Hands seized her head and dragged it nearer to the pane.

Todd ran to the window. He looked at Ellen, but went for Barbara first. Wrapping himself around her, he tried to pull—and was enveloped by hands, too.

Barbara found it difficult to discern words amid the rumbling sea of insults and periodic shouts, but one somewhat familiar voice was closest to her ear. "Got that dress at Wal-Mart, didn't cha?" it said to her.

"I'm not even wearing a dress, you—" She slapped a fist to her mouth.

An asshole gave Todd's scalp an Indian burn. "Resist it," he shouted through his pain. "They're not worth your anger!"

But there were so many hands, pulling at her arms and shoulders and hair, slapping at her back. Giving in to them just seemed easier, if not more right.

"Stay strong, Barbara!"

"I can't!" she cried.

Todd strained to pull himself forward; he was almost free. "*You must!*"

At that moment, an asshole hand spread two fingers and poked her in the eyes. "Go fu—" she began.

"Be an asshole to Ellen!" Todd shouted over her. "It's the only way!"

Suddenly, Barbara had hope. She turned to Ellen, whose mouth was opening and closing like that of a goldfish, body writhing against the onslaught of hands. "You're a total cunt rag!" Barbara screamed. "Instead of beating Harold's ass, you should be grateful for him!"

Though Ellen said nothing—and couldn't say anything because the hand of an asshole had wrapped itself tightly around her mouth—Barbara imagined she wanted to ask, "*why?*"

"Because no other man would want you, you stupid, ugly bitch!"

With a roar, Ellen shook free and launched herself at Barbara. The hands held on until the combined weight dragged both women down and they fell rolling to the floor.

Ellen landed a blow to Barbara's face. "Who's the ugly bitch?" she shrieked. "You'll be the ugly bitch!" She struck again.

Barbara spat. A sliver of white enamel adhered to her bottom lip for a second before falling. But she barely felt pain as she imagined the blood inside Ellen, and the veins, tendons and muscles concealed by skin. Barbara intended to see these things, laid out before her in glistening ribbons and chunks, like a buffet.

Before Barbara could act, Ellen flew from atop her and, upon hitting the wall, made a sound like *oomph*. Todd bent down, helped Barbara to her feet. Ellen stood up, approached her, but Todd brandished his pole. "Fight some other time!" he said.

Ellen backed down, though she didn't take her eyes off

Barbara. "Later," she mouthed.

"Make a date," Barbara mouthed back, then spat another chunk of tooth.

Todd looked around. "Where's Harold? That fucker better not be back in the clock!"

"Here I am," he said softly, rising from his hiding place behind the sofa.

"Good," said Todd. "We need everyone here. Believe it or not, we've still got time to think."

"*Time to think*?" Ellen snorted. "After what just—"

Todd didn't let her finish. "It's packed tight out there. I doubt those in front can do much more than wave their fucking arms, and it's going to take a lot of maneuvering for others to get within ten feet of an opening."

At that moment, all hands retracted simultaneously. There was the sound of barked commands, falling bodies and retreating footsteps.

"What was that guy saying?" Ellen asked.

"He said you're an—"

"*Not now*, Barbara!" Todd turned to Ellen. "Don't know. Couldn't understand him."

Harold sounded almost joyful. "I—I think he must have told them all to leave!"

Todd just shook his head.

Suddenly: grunting and a host of heavy footsteps, followed by a *bang* that seemed to shake the whole house. Dust drifted down from the ceiling.

"Shit!" said Todd. "That must be a battering ram!"

Another *bang*. Boards covering the window splintered. A third *bang*, and those on the bottom and left side were pushed away from the wall. In moments, the window was free of obstruction. Assholes approached it, some forcing past others or climbing over the sea of heads in a frenzied attempt to be first on the scene. They packed themselves by the window, so many there appeared to be no gaps between them. Ones in front struggled to enter.

"Barbara!" Todd shouted as he sprinted to a pile of tools and seized an armload of them. "Grab as many boards and nails as you can! Run to the den!"

The first asshole squeezed past the rest and entered the living room. He was a filthy, hulking man, reminiscent of a pig. He carried a woman's severed head by the hair. Barbara imagined he might have ripped it off her neck with his hands alone.

Harold was nearest to the asshole; he had nothing in his arms. Todd pitched his ass-ramming pole to him. "Take this! You know what you have to do!"

"No! Please god, no!"

The asshole sniffed the air, grunted like an animal.

"Kill that asshole!"

"I—I…"

The asshole set his gaze on Barbara, who was frozen at the sight of him. He licked his lips and dropped the head. It rolled to a stop near the pole by Harold's feet.

"Do it or we're all dead!"

Harold gulped, picked up the pole, jumped over the head and ran up behind the asshole. Closing his eyes, grimacing, he sent the pole in an upward arc that tore through the thing's pants, but went no farther than an enema. The asshole groaned. He tried to turn and swipe bloody, ham-like fists at Harold.

"You gotta force it up there, Harold! All the way!"

"I'm trying! Oh god, I'm trying!" He strained. The pole penetrated deeper. The asshole's body made bubbly, popping sounds. Barbara imagined meat tearing, organs bursting. She wanted to be sick.

The asshole fell twitching to the floor, but more seeped through the window.

"What are you staring at?" Todd shouted to everyone. "Get in the room!"

Ellen had to pull Harold inside.

154

CHAPTER THIRTY-NINE

Barbara kept her back against the door. In her mind, it made it more secure.

Todd congratulated Harold. "There. You did it. Are you proud of yourself?"

He could only shake, mutter occasionally.

"I understand, man," Todd said. "The first time is always the most intense."

Harold turned away, walked past his wife and to a corner. He fell down into it, looked at his hands as he turned them over and over.

Barbara was watching Harold. Though it felt wrong to be glad someone else had to kill the asshole, she was glad just the same. She turned then to the bodies beneath the sheet on the sofa. At least Billy and Linda hadn't had to see them again.

"It's okay for now," Todd said to the room in general. "But that bottleneck isn't going to last—"

The door rattled hard. Though it didn't sound like many feet were kicking it, one set apparently belonged to a strong asshole, and the door nearly jumped out of its frame. Barbara bolted from it, torn from her thoughts as Todd approached with boards and hammers and nails and immediately set to work. Quickly, Barbara returned to offer assistance and, in time, even Ellen lifted a board or two.

Harold sat rocking back and forth, mumbling to himself on the floor.

CHAPTER FORTY

Todd stepped back and regarded the door. Assholes behind it still kicked, but the frame no longer shook and hinges no longer rattled. "It's as secure as it'll ever be," he said.

Harold had been mumbling in the corner, though no one heard him until the hammering stopped. "I—I stuck a pole up—up somebody's ass," he said to himself. "I—I killed him."

"Yes," Todd said. "Again, good job."

Suddenly, he seemed aware of others in the room. He shook his head back and forth. "No! Bad job! Very, very bad job! I—I should…kill myself!"

"Why?" Todd asked.

"Because it would be easier. And—and we should all do the same!"

Todd furrowed his brows. "And how do you propose we pull that off?"

"I don't know!" Harold's eyes scanned the room and fell upon the hammer in Todd's hand. "With that," he said, pointing.

"You want us to bash each other over the head with a hammer? Really? And what's the last person going to do?"

"Guess I didn't really think it through. I—"

"You bet you didn't!" He clenched his fists. "We have to collect ourselves, you idiot, not kill ourselves!"

"We're fucked, okay!" He cupped his head in his palms. When he spoke again, his voice held little power. "We've just got to admit that."

Todd bent down, glared intently at Harold. "We're not fucked until I say we're fucked."

"Then say we're fucked!"

"I agree with my husband," Ellen said. "Say we're fucked."

Barbara sighed inwardly. She'd expected something like this. More bickering. More fighting. Even at the end. She found herself wondering if assholes, once they all broke through, would be able to tell themselves apart from non-assholes.

And, as much as she hated to admit it, Barbara found herself in agreement with Harold and Ellen.

"I don't know; maybe they have a point," she said to Todd. "I mean, where else are we going to go? The clock? God knows where that leads. Maybe we should just…" She let her words die away and cast her gaze to the floor.

Barbara glanced up when Todd approached her. She didn't like the look on his face. "Never talk like that, Barbara! There's nothing worse than becoming an asshole!"

"At least I won't remember who I was; nobody'll morn me."

His angry look faded, became one of concern. "I'm sorry for yelling, but you can't stop now. As long as—"

"Don't listen to him. He has no—"

"Shut up, Ellen!" Todd faced Barbara again, stepped a little closer to her. "As long as people like us exist, we spit in the assholes' faces. We defy them and give them reason to fear."

It seemed to Barbara that he'd gotten it backwards. "I think we're the scared ones, Todd."

"Sure we are, but why would they want to eradicate us if we didn't pose a threat? It's because we stand for something they don't."

"But they've got—"

"And even if we don't survive, others like us will, and our *spirit* will be with them. I believe this, Barbara."

"*But they've got a battering ram, Todd!*"

"I don't care if they've got a legion of tanks! We can't let that spirit die."

If only for Todd's sake, she decided to play Sisyphus for the night. "Okay, sure. Let's keep going."

He smiled thinly, took a few steps back and, for a moment, contemplated the tools he'd brought. "I believe I'm going to drive a hole in the wall, near the ceiling," he said. "We can climb out if we have to. By that time, maybe there'll be more of them inside than out there."

"A hole in the wall?" Ellen retorted. "How stupid can you—"

The clock door swung open behind them. A man in an old military outfit staggered out, clutching his head and moaning. He was middle-aged, of slender build, and had dark, oily hair and a tiny moustache.

"*Wo bin ich?*" said the man as though his mouth were full. Rheumy eyes focused on nothing in particular. Knees shook, so he placed an equally shaky hand on the wall to act as a brace.

"No, baby, no!" Ellen shouted. "Stay in the clock!"

"*Baby?*" Barbara spat. "He's your daughter?"

"I know what you're thinking, but she's not Hitler! She's just—just an impersonator!" She turned to Harold then. "You were supposed to give her the sedatives last!"

"Well, I was—I—"

"Too busy sniveling, weren't you!"

Todd shook his head. "I was pretty sure she was an asshole—but come on!" His voice began to waver. "I should smack you both."

The German finally took notice. "*Amerikaner!*" he cried. Pulling his hand from the wall, he spun backwards, towards the clock, and almost tripped on his feet.

Hefting his pole, Todd raced for the man. Ellen raced for Todd, reaching him just as the clock door closed behind the German.

"No!" She grabbed Todd's shoulder. "You will not put that up my daughter's ass!"

Todd pushed her away, kept going. Harold ran after both of them. Barbara figured she'd better start running too.

CHAPTER FORTY-ONE

It was pitch black in the clock, everyone running too fast to use lighters. Barbara had no idea whose footsteps were whose. Did a set just pass her? Was there another behind her? Was Todd going to ram a pole up her ass by mistake?

She heard someone trip somewhere ahead of her, and then a voice, sounded like it was cursing, but not in English. Seconds later, she ran up against someone's back. Felt wide. Had to be Todd.

A lighter ignited. The German had fallen unceremoniously to the floor, face-first. "*Ich fühle mich krank*," he moaned.

Todd lifted a foot to plant atop the German's back, but thought better of it. Instead, he just raised the pole, took aim.

Lost in the dark, Ellen had gotten in front of everyone else. She saw the light, turned and jumped over Hitler. Then she tried to jump Todd. Against Barbara's every maternal instinct, she brandished her own pole in his defense while simultaneously trying to ignite her lighter.

Todd addressed Ellen. "Now, as much as you might not want to admit it, your daughter is an asshole. A lot of daughters are assholes today. Terrible, but that's just the way it is, and you've got to come to terms with that fact."

"*No!*"

"Just admit it. Say your daughter is an asshole."

"I can't!"

He lifted the pole higher. "Say it!"

"If I do it, you'll kill her!"

"I'll kill the asshole anyway! Say it!"

"My daughter is…is…"

He began to tremble. "*Now!*"

159

"An asshole! But I can't let you stake her! She's all I ever loved and all I've got left!"

Finally, Barbara recognized some humanity in Ellen. She felt sorry for her, but still brandished the pole.

Harold, huffing and puffing, finally reached them. "Just—just let the man do it, honey. Please."

He tried to embrace her, but Ellen pushed him away. "I knew you were stupid," she said, "but I didn't know you were evil, too!"

"But he's right. That's not our daughter. There's no trace of her in there, and we've got to finally admit that."

"We don't have to admit *anything*! Not to these people!"

"Do you think this is easy for me, Ellen? But it's Hitler, honey! Fucking Hitler!"

"You protected her, too!" Ellen screamed. "And she's an impersonator, damn it!"

"I protected her, yeah," Harold shot back. "But only because of you!"

"If you want this so much, why not do it yourself? Go on! Stick the pole right up your daughter's ass!"

Todd thought for a moment before extending the pole to Harold. He reached for it.

She paled. "I wasn't being serious!"

"No, I'm going to do this." Harold gripped the pole. It shook in his hands. "She used to be my daughter, so I should be the one. Just—just don't watch me, Ellen. Turn your back! Leave!"

Todd flicked his lighter again. "Make your aim true," he said to Harold.

Ellen spun around. She ran screaming down the hall and out the clock.

Barbara didn't want to look, either. It didn't matter if it was Hitler. She couldn't take seeing another pole go up another ass, so she ran in the opposite direction of Ellen into blackness that seemed infinite. She kept running until a rock tripped her and she tumbled to the floor. Barbara

160

waited about a minute. Then she got up, brushed herself off and turned back the way she'd arrived.

When she neared the site, she saw Todd's lighter illuminating the dead German. She refused to look at the corpse more than once. Harold wasn't there. Barbara asked where he'd gone.

"He's outside with Ellen," Todd replied. "Figured I'd give them a few minutes to sort things out before I went back."

"Good id—" She closed her mouth as her eyes fell on the pole Todd carried, and the blood that coated it, dripping down to his fingers.

Noting her stare, Todd turned the pole clean end up.

CHAPTER FORTY-TWO

Ellen was prying the last two boards from the door when Barbara and Todd reentered the den. Harold was on the floor, motionless, his head twisted at an unnatural angle, a little trickle of blood flowing from his bottom lip. Barbara ran to Harold, but it was clear she could do nothing for him. "Why did you do it!" she shouted.

"He took everything from me!" She pulled off another board; the door began to shake and rattle. "So I took everything from him!"

Todd reached Ellen. He spun her around, smacked her, first with his left hand, then with his right.

She spat in Todd's face. "Fuck you, child killer!"

Todd threw her to the floor. "Hold her, Barbara," he said, and hefted one of the fallen boards and a hammer.

Ellen tried to get up, but Barbara pushed her down and got on the floor. She wrapped her arms around Ellen's and pinned them behind her back before knotting her legs around the woman's waist. Ellen twisted and squirmed. "Let go of me, you bitch!" she shouted, but Barbara held her tighter as Todd nailed the board.

The door facing began to separate from the wall. The board pushed out. Todd kept hammering it, even as nails continued to pop up.

Ellen reared back and hit her head against Barbara's. Barbara swooned a bit, but didn't let go until Ellen hit her harder. Barbara felt a starburst of pain in her skull and cried out. Ellen squirmed free from her grasp. Picking up the crowbar, she rushed to the door.

She hit Todd in the back. As he fell forward, but caught himself against a wall, Ellen wedged the crowbar between the only board and the door. In a matter of seconds, she'd flung it to the carpet.

One of the hinges cracked. The top half of the door sagged inward. Todd pushed away from the wall, wrenched the crowbar from Ellen's hands and knocked her to the side. He pressed himself against the door. Ellen began to slap at him, hard, but he held his ground until the combined weight of the assholes proved too much for him.

The door fell in completely. Todd and Ellen moved just in time to avoid being smashed under it. Hands entered, followed by legs and feet and bodies. One was a drunk British soccer fan, pint glass in hand. His shirt read, *Property of Shitwanshire Rugby League.*

Still on the floor, Barbara relived memories from the mall until a hand grabbed her shoulder. *An asshole hand?* she wondered distantly. No, Todd's hand, and it got her up and pulled her toward him and made her run back to the clock.

Ellen remained at the door. Assholes—more and more by the second—clamored around her, insulting her and touching her inappropriately. She took the crowbar to the closest one, caved in its skull. She tripped another and stomped its face. "I don't care!" she shouted, then laughed. "Make me one of—" Words dissolved. She clutched her head, scrunched her face and became a fat black lady in a muumuu.

CHAPTER FORTY-THREE

They ran through the guts of the clock. Barbara flicked her lighter. No way to keep a flame, but the sparks provided brief and flickering illumination.

The strobing effect began to disorient her. She stopped flicking the lighter, but her head still swam. Past the spot where they'd found Billy and Linda, sound seemed to Doppler unnaturally. She couldn't tell if the sound of footfalls were echoes of her own or those of assholes trailing her. She turned once, but it was too dark to see.

Minutes later, Todd began to flick his own lighter. "Start slowing down!" he said.

Barbara imagined the assholes might have gotten ahead of them, perhaps found a secret way in. Still, she slowed. Not long afterwards, Todd came to a halt.

"What is it?" she asked.

"Take a look at this." He ignited the lighter, moving it up and down, gradually showing her the entirety of a heavy wooden door, covered in moss. Short and squat, its handle was a forged iron ring.

Todd reached out to open it. Barbara grabbed his hand. "I don't know if you should," she said.

"Perhaps not, but it looks like our only choice."

Barbara released his hand, and Todd turned the knob.

The door opened into a bland bedroom. In fact, it seemed to Barbara that they'd finally found an upstairs chamber. She tried to close the door to the clock, but found there was no door.

Suddenly: a clatter at the window. Barbara hastened to it and saw three or four assholes scaling a ladder. One had nearly reached the top.

Todd pushed her aside, opened the pane and gave

the ladder a shove. Assholes fell screaming to the ground. Upon writhing a bit and dusting themselves off, they re-erected the ladder and started climbing again.

Barbara ran to the bedroom door, turned the knob that locked it. She heard the sound of assholes—hundreds, if not thousands of them—banging around, knocking things over. Wouldn't be long before an army found them. Maybe assholes wouldn't see any doors upstairs, but she imagined they would. They'd find thousands and thousands of doors where she'd found none, and all would lead to the room with Todd.

Barbara went to a dresser, searched its drawers.

"What are you looking for?" Todd asked. Then he pulled the assholes' ladder up through the window and into the room.

"Maybe there's a gun here, too."

Todd leaned his weight against the drawers, closing them. "You sound like Harold. Stop it."

"But—"

"I don't want to hear that." He looked into her eyes then, and kept looking. "Besides, I just thought of something."

She couldn't imagine what Todd was considering. In her estimation, there was nothing more to do but await the inevitable.

"I have no idea if this'll work," he said, brows knitted, "but it makes sense. Tell me, Barbara, what's the one act these assholes can't comprehend?"

She shrugged.

"An act of love."

"What?"

"An act of love. And if they break in and see us engaged in one, it might repel them."

Across the hall, a window shattered. "I'm still not getting you."

Todd moved in closer. "You're a beautiful woman, Barbara; I think you know this."

She backed up. "I—I don't know what I know!"

"It would be my honor to make love to you."

Soon, Barbara was against a wall. "But we've only known each other a day!"

Todd advanced. "This day is unlike any other."

"Really, Todd, you're a good-looking guy, and it's not that I don't—"

"We can sit back and let ourselves become assholes or we can do something. I don't want to rape you, Barbara. I want us to survive, at any cost." He paused, thought a bit. "Perhaps we can start with a kiss."

She thought a bit, too. Finally: "Just a kiss?"

He nodded, gestured to the bed. She followed him and took a seat on it. Dropping his ass-ramming pole, Todd leaned over to kiss her. Barbara turned her head to the left.

"But I saw some assholes outside earlier," she said. "They were having sex, and it didn't stop anything."

"There was no love in their act, Barbara."

It sounded like a bunch of assholes were clomping up the stairs.

"Do you think you can love me?" he continued.

"I, uh—"

"Do you? It's important."

Though the situation was awkward, she found herself wanting Todd. Too much time had passed since she'd been with a man, her temper driving all of them away before anything real could happen. Now here was one who wanted her—a strong, attractive and resourceful man, and, more than likely, the last she'd ever see.

But did she love him?

Regardless, Barbara nodded her consent, slid quickly out of her clothes and moved backwards until her head rested atop the pillow.

Todd stood, removed his shirt, dropped his pants and crawled atop her. She tried to focus on his looming face, not the sound of more glass shattering and footsteps just outside the room.

He stroked her cheek. His hand felt warm and reassuring. Barbara relaxed her shoulders and allowed Todd's tongue to enter her, then his penis.

Endorphins kicked in. Suddenly, Barbara could pretend she was somewhere else, somewhere nice, and this wasn't a man she'd met earlier in the day. He was her soul mate, and everything would be fine because he loved her and she loved him. They might even share a post-coital smoke, go out to eat later, take in a movie…do something—anything—that didn't involve becoming an asshole.

The sound of a cracking door split open her fantasy world. Todd didn't seem to notice, but Barbara turned, saw wood fall away and the bedroom start to fill with assholes—cheerleaders, businessmen, skinheads, preachers, teachers—the whole gamut. Then the window broke. More poured through the gap.

"Todd," she said. "Todd, they're—"

"I know."

She watched them, even as Todd continued to make love to her. They formed a bubble by the door, about a dozen in the room and who knew how many clustered behind, just waiting for their moment. But they didn't say or do anything. Hands hung by their sides. Faces were slack-jawed, eyes dazed.

Todd pulled out just as her orgasm was imminent.

"What? I was—"

"Can't now," Todd told her. "Have to conserve it." He arose quickly.

"Todd, where are you—"

He reached over, pulled her to his side of the bed. Just as she got to her feet, he said, "Make out with me, as passionately as you can. Start walking backwards as you do."

"But—"

"Don't worry. I'll be your eyes."

Barbara grabbed Todd's ass and kneaded it. She pressed

her lips against his, pried them open with her tongue. Then they started walking.

She found it hard, matching Todd's steps while making out. A tongue was apt to slip from the other mouth; kisses were likely to miss their target. Each time these things happened, a previously docile asshole started to look hungry.

"Don't look at them," Todd said, his hands cupping her breasts.

Barbara closed her eyes, and they continued down the hall, assholes falling away, parting like a sea of reeds.

It felt like they had walked and made out for an hour. Whether Todd was trying to find the stairs or the hole that led to the kitchen, Barbara couldn't say. The hallway kept bending, circling; it didn't seem to have a stable axis.

How long could Todd continue French kissing her? How long could she maintain a sense of passion? For however long it took, she imagined.

Barbara had come to realize that she loved Todd, perhaps more than she'd ever loved a man, and—though it would add a whole new level of awkwardness—she wished Billy and Linda were around to do this, too.

Finally, they found the top of the stairs. Todd didn't hesitate to start down them, nor did his tongue leave her mouth. Assholes who were ascending began descending backwards.

Todd and Barbara reached the bottom, and he was inside her again. Barbara gasped at the sudden intrusion and almost tripped. Todd's manhood flopped loose.

"I can't walk and do that!" she cried.

Assholes heard this. Eyes clearing, they advanced.

"Then get on me. I'll carry you."

Barbara jumped, and he caught her. She wrapped her legs around his back. Todd resumed his thrusts as they exited the front door, now just a hole in the wall. Assholes on the porch moved to the steps. Assholes on the steps moved to the yard.

The night air was cool against Barbara's skin. The floodlights beat down mercilessly, made her feel like she was being filmed. She tried to bury that sensation and focus instead on Todd and her love for him until brightness faded and they entered the woods behind the house. Within twenty feet, darkness had enveloped them fully.

Perhaps assholes lurked behind trees or rocks, concealed by shadow, but she couldn't think about that, not when the first orgasm of the night seized her and rippled through her body in waves.

CHAPTER FORTY-FOUR

It was early morning.

Barbara awoke beside Todd. Her memories of the woods were of near-constant sex in darkness that verged on negative space. Things were different now. She saw they'd passed out by a stream that ran through a wooded valley bounded by steep, rounded hills. In an apple tree just above them, birds sang. A breeze rustled leaves.

Again, Barbara closed her eyes, focused on these sounds and imagined the valley was the only real place on Earth. After a few minutes, it struck her that, for the first time in years, her initial thought upon awakening hadn't involved cigarettes.

She was glad for this; she didn't want one. Maybe if she and Todd stayed together, kissing and making love whenever necessary, they'd survive and teach others to do the same. The world would be filled not with assholes, but with fuckers who loved.

In the long run, that seemed more important to her than cigarettes.

Todd opened his eyes. He remained silent and motionless for a minute or two, looking up at the sky and the apples that hung over his head. Then he turned to Barbara. "Hungry?" he asked.

She felt no need to conceal herself. "Yes," she said.

Todd arose, reached up and plucked two apples from the tree. Barbara bit into her apple. Never before had she tasted one so sweet. She didn't know if this was due to actual sweetness, or the fact she hadn't expected to taste an apple again.

"We made it; by god." Todd took a bite of his own. "There was a time I thought I'd never get to say that."

The revelation shocked Barbara. "You seemed so confident."

"I had to seem that way, for you, for the others." He sat beside her then. His feet dangled in the stream. "Even Ellen and Harold."

"I owe you everything, Todd."

"I think we probably owe each other." He finished his apple, tossed away the core and leaned over to kiss her. Barbara offered no resistance. She welcomed the taste of his lips and tongue.

"Excuse me for a second," he said upon pulling away. "There's something I really need to do."

"What?"

Todd smiled. "Just watch. Maybe you'll want to join me." He turned, walked a few paces and extended his middle finger. "Fuck you, assholes!" he shouted suddenly. "Fuck your mothers, too!"

Barbara grinned. Maybe she would join him.

"We won!" he continued. "Do you hear that? *We won!*"

In the distance, an asshole popped up from behind a rock. "Yeah, I heard that!" He jumped up and down, cavorted. "Ha ha! I heard that!"

Todd rasped. Stumbling backwards, he almost fell over Barbara.

Fear wanted to paralyze her, but she fought against it and made herself stand. They couldn't take Todd. She wouldn't allow it.

He clutched his head, began to convulse.

She held him, stroked the back of his head and kissed him, long and deep. If love had gotten them out of the house, maybe it could prevent his transformation, too.

But there was less of Todd to hug as his body thinned out. Skin lightened; hair lengthened. It became blond and wavy. Clothes appeared atop him—a crisp, black suit. Still Barbara held him, clinging onto hope.

"Hello, Barbara," said a new voice.

She searched the asshole's pale blue eyes. "Todd? Are you still there?"

"No, he's not. But I was chosen to come to you specifically, to make you an offer." He stepped back from Barbara, straightened his tie. "You know, not every asshole hangs around farmhouses all day. Some are leaders."

Todd was gone. Todd wasn't coming back. Rage blossomed. She wanted to tear the asshole apart with her hands, fling his flesh to the ground for worms to eat. But she refused to give him the satisfaction. No matter what happened, she couldn't let him see her change.

"You can maintain your humanity if you want," he continued, "and I know you do."

"What are you saying?" she growled.

"Few humans remain. Powerful assholes such as myself will require slaves."

She turned from him, struck the apple tree and kept striking it, even as her knuckles cracked and bled.

"Perhaps you dislike serving a master." A glossy brochure appeared in his hand. The cover showed a group of twenty people bound to chairs in a ring beneath a big-top tent. Bleachers were full of cheering assholes. "Why not become part of the Circus, then? You'll be amongst your own kind, performing daily for the masses. Your hands and legs will be tied and your vocal cords severed, of course—but you'll still be human."

"Hands tied? Vocal cords severed?" Barbara said. Then she cackled.

"Well, we can't have you transform, can we? What fun is there in being an asshole if there're no people around to be assholes to?"

Barbara turned back to the tree and resumed hitting it.

He sighed. "Your answer is *no*, then." A butcher knife appeared in his hand, huge and serrated. "Here. Stab me

172

as hard and as often as you want."

She regarded the knife, imagined it going in and out of his body and the blood that would rise in an arc from it, splattering the ground and trees and—even better—her face. But then the asshole would arise, smooth out his jacket and walk away. There was no joy in imagining that.

He shook the knife. Barbara didn't look at it. She just stood there, shredded knuckles coloring one side of her pants red.

"Still fighting, I see." The asshole lowered the knife. "But there's no war to wage; it's already been waged, silently, for thousands of years. Tell me, how much change do you think is possible in a world without assholes?"

Barbara didn't know what to say, what to think.

"No change, Barbara. No change at all." Again, he held out the knife. "Just take it."

She reached out, accepted the knife, turned it over in her hands and saw her reflection in its blade.

The asshole smiled, unbuttoned his jacket and pushed out his chest. "Start wherever," he said. "You can even go for the face."

She lifted the knife. Rather than plunging it into the asshole, she threw it into the creek. "Go away," she said, trying not to scream, to remain even keeled despite the pressure that threatened to explode her. "Just leave."

"Well, don't say I didn't give you a chance." He gestured with a forward sweep of his hand.

From the tops of both hills, a seemingly unbroken line of assholes emerged. The well-dressed asshole waved up at them. "I'll be on my way now," he said to Barbara, turning as the line advanced. Another line appeared just behind the first, and another behind that, and then a thousand more. The woods swarmed with assholes. They bore down on her and ate up the rest of the world in their wake. No grass. No trees. No stream. No air.

They smashed up against her—a living tide—hands and faces all over and around her, flapping lips saying so many things the resulting noise sounded more like ocean waves than speech. Those waves tried to carry her away to a place where there was nothing but rage and blood.

But she couldn't travel to those shores. She closed her eyes instead, imagining herself clad in a suit of armor on an immense battlefield, stabbing with her noble pole, *Excelsior*. She struck at an asshole, but only pants were penetrated, and the asshole charged—eyes wild, teeth like sharpened points. Barbara dodged, came up behind it and drove *Excelsior* deep into its ass. But she wasn't finished. She shoved until the tip shot from its mouth, for she was now Queen Barbara Victorious, slaying the asshole.

But that was mere fantasy. She could say and do nothing. As usual, Todd had been right; this *was* the ultimate test, and she'd pass. She'd pass without hitting an asshole, much less ramming a pole up a single ass. That, after all, was a form of failure. She'd pass if she had to go insane first, and she would, undoubtedly.

Barbara opened her eyes. Saw so many assholes they seemed to be of one huge and amorphous self. She tried to move, but couldn't. Her feet were off the ground, her body suspended between countless others.

Madness seemed close, but rage so much closer. She relished the sweet *plonk* as her fist collided with a banker's head and the crack of cartilage as a rapist's nose turned to putty. Those sounds seemed so much like music, music she could dance and sway to, all day long and all across the valley and over everyone's fat fucking faces. Twirl, twirl, twirl—she was just like a ballerina before she realized her feet and fists were aflutter.

And then she was out of the room, out of the house, up in the sky. Dancing in the stars now, and then past them to a place beyond celestial bodies, sight and sound.

Figures like flames of many color erupted in the night-that-wasn't-a-night. They attracted one another, burned brighter and blended, forming one super body imbued with a presence all-knowing and all-invasive. It appeared almost human, but too big for Barbara to wrap her mind around and see fully. The one thing she knew: It wanted to strip her clean.

Her knees bent. She found herself bowing before what could only be The God of All Assholes, the highest of the high.

"Come to me, my daughter, with whom I'm well pleased," It said, and Barbara stood, walked to It, vestiges of her former self peeling away with every step, falling like papers that burst into flames and were forgotten. At that moment, she felt connected to something huge, earth-shaping, and unlike so many others things, It welcomed her into Itself.

She tingled as she entered the Godhead. Then her body became a non-body, moving in fluid, serpentine ways no fixed human form could duplicate. She felt a billion fellow souls writhing there with her, becoming refined, being made pure before returning to Earth to do the Good Work—bringers of a brave new tomorrow.

ABOUT THE AUTHOR

Kevin L. Donihe, perhaps the world's oldest living wombat, resides in the hills of Tennessee. He has published five other books via Eraserhead Press. His short fiction and poetry has appeared in The Mammoth Book of Legal Thrillers, ChiZine, The Cafe Irreal, Poe's Progeny, Bathtub Gin, Not One of Us, Dreams and Nightmares, Electric Velocipede, Bust Down the Door and Eat All the Chickens, and many other venues. He also edits the Bare Bone anthology series for Raw Dog Screaming Press, a story from which was reprinted in The Mammoth Book of Best New Horror 13.

Visit him online at myspace.com/kevindonihe

Bizarro books

CATALOG   SPRING 2010

Bizarro Books publishes under the following imprints:

www.rawdogscreamingpress.com

www.eraserheadpress.com

www.afterbirthbooks.com

www.swallowdownpress.com

For all your Bizarro needs visit:

WWW.BIZARROCENTRAL.COM

Introduce yourselves to the bizarro genre and all of its authors with the Bizarro Starter Kit series. Each volume features short novels and short stories by ten of the leading bizarro authors, designed to give you a perfect sampling of the genre for only $5 plus shipping.

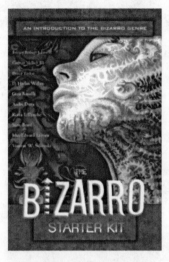

BB-0X1
"The Bizarro Starter Kit" (Orange)

Featuring D. Harlan Wilson, Carlton Mellick III, Jeremy Robert Johnson, Kevin L Donihe, Gina Ranalli, Andre Duza, Vincent W. Sakowski, Steve Beard, John Edward Lawson, and Bruce Taylor.

236 pages $5

BB-0X2
"The Bizarro Starter Kit" (Blue)

Featuring Ray Fracalossy, Jeremy C. Shipp, Jordan Krall, Mykle Hansen, Andersen Prunty, Eckhard Gerdes, Bradley Sands, Steve Aylett, Christian TeBordo, and Tony Rauch.

244 pages $5

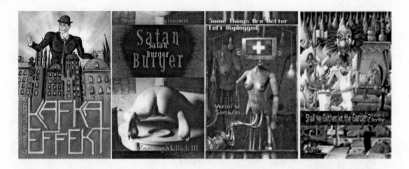

BB-001 "The Kafka Effekt" D. Harlan Wilson - A collection of forty-four irreal short stories loosely written in the vein of Franz Kafka, with more than a pinch of William S. Burroughs sprinkled on top. **211 pages $14**

BB-002 "Satan Burger" Carlton Mellick III - The cult novel that put Carlton Mellick III on the map ... Six punks get jobs at a fast food restaurant owned by the devil in a city violently overpopulated by surreal alien cultures. **236 pages $14**

BB-003 "Some Things Are Better Left Unplugged" Vincent Sakwoski - Join The Man and his Nemesis, the obese tabby, for a nightmare roller coaster ride into this postmodern fantasy. **152 pages $10**

BB-004 "Shall We Gather At the Garden?" Kevin L Donihe - Donihe's Debut novel. Midgets take over the world, The Church of Lionel Richie vs. The Church of the Byrds, plant porn and more! **244 pages $14**

BB-005 "Razor Wire Pubic Hair" Carlton Mellick III - A genderless humandildo is purchased by a razor dominatrix and brought into her nightmarish world of bizarre sex and mutilation. **176 pages $11**

BB-006 "Stranger on the Loose" D. Harlan Wilson - The fiction of Wilson's 2nd collection is planted in the soil of normalcy, but what grows out of that soil is a dark, witty, otherworldly jungle... **228 pages $14**

BB-007 "The Baby Jesus Butt Plug" Carlton Mellick III - Using clones of the Baby Jesus for anal sex will be the hip sex fetish of the future. **92 pages $10**

BB-008 "Fishyfleshed" Carlton Mellick III - The world of the past is an illogical flatland lacking in dimension and color, a sick-scape of crispy squid people wandering the desert for no apparent reason. **260 pages $14**

BB-009 "Dead Bitch Army" Andre Duza - Step into a world filled with racist teenagers, cannibals, 100 warped Uncle Sams, automobiles with razor-sharp teeth, living graffiti, and a pissed-off zombie bitch out for revenge. **344 pages $16**

BB-010 "The Menstruating Mall" Carlton Mellick III - "The Breakfast Club meets Chopping Mall as directed by David Lynch." - Brian Keene **212 pages $12**

BB-011 "Angel Dust Apocalypse" Jeremy Robert Johnson - Meth-heads, man-made monsters, and murderous Neo-Nazis. "Seriously amazing short stories..." - Chuck Palahniuk, author of Fight Club **184 pages $11**

BB-012 "Ocean of Lard" Kevin L Donihe / Carlton Mellick III - A parody of those old Choose Your Own Adventure kid's books about some very odd pirates sailing on a sea made of animal fat. **176 pages $12**

BB-013 "Last Burn in Hell" John Edward Lawson - From his lurid angst-affair with a lesbian music diva to his ascendance as unlikely pop icon the one constant for Kenrick Brimley, official state prison gigolo, is he's got no clue what he's doing. **172 pages $14**

BB-014 "Tangerinephant" Kevin Dole 2 - TV-obsessed aliens have abducted Michael Tangerinephant in this bizarro combination of science fiction, satire, and surrealism. **164 pages $11**

BB-015 "Foop!" Chris Genoa - Strange happenings are going on at Dactyl, Inc, the world's first and only time travel tourism company.

"A surreal pie in the face!" - Christopher Moore **300 pages $14**

BB-016 "Spider Pie" Alyssa Sturgill - A one-way trip down a rabbit hole inhabited by sexual deviants and friendly monsters, fairytale beginnings and hideous endings. **104 pages $11**

BB-017 "The Unauthorized Woman" Efrem Emerson - Enter the world of the inner freak, a landscape populated by the pre-dead and morticioners, by cockroaches and 300-lb robots. **104 pages $11**

BB-018 "Fugue XXIX" Forrest Aguirre - Tales from the fringe of speculative literary fiction where innovative minds dream up the future's uncharted territories while mining forgotten treasures of the past. **220 pages $16**

BB-019 "Pocket Full of Loose Razorblades" John Edward Lawson - A collection of dark bizarro stories. From a giant rectum to a foot-fungus factory to a girl with a biforked tongue. **190 pages $13**

BB-020 "Punk Land" Carlton Mellick III - In the punk version of Heaven, the anarchist utopia is threatened by corporate fascism and only Goblin, Mortician's sperm, and a blue-mohawked female assassin named Shark Girl can stop them. **284 pages $15**

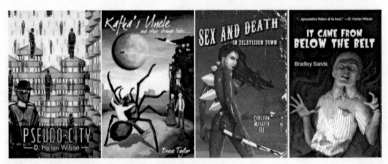

BB-021 "Pseudo-City" D. Harlan Wilson - Pseudo-City exposes what waits in the bathroom stall, under the manhole cover and in the corporate boardroom, all in a way that can only be described as mind-bogglingly irreal. **220 pages $16**

BB-022 "Kafka's Uncle and Other Strange Tales" Bruce Taylor - Anslenot and his giant tarantula (tormentor? fri-end?) wander a desecrated world in this novel and collection of stories from Mr. Magic Realism Himself. **348 pages $17**

BB-023 "Sex and Death In Television Town" Carlton Mellick III - In the old west, a gang of hermaphrodite gunslingers take refuge from a demon plague in Telos: a town where its citizens have televisions instead of heads. **184 pages $12**

BB-024 "It Came From Below The Belt" Bradley Sands - What can Grover Goldstein do when his severed, sentient penis forces him to return to high school and help it win the presidential election? **204 pages $13**

BB-025 **"Sick: An Anthology of Illness" John Lawson, editor** - These Sick stories are horrendous and hilarious dissections of creative minds on the scalpel's edge. **296 pages $16**

BB-026 **"Tempting Disaster" John Lawson, editor** - A shocking and alluring anthology from the fringe that examines our culture's obsession with taboos. **260 pages $16**

BB-027 **"Siren Promised" Jeremy Robert Johnson & Alan M Clark** - Nominated for the Bram Stoker Award. A potent mix of bad drugs, bad dreams, brutal bad guys, and surreal/incredible art by Alan M. Clark. **190 pages $13**

BB-028 **"Chemical Gardens" Gina Ranalli** - Ro and punk band Green is the Enemy find Kreepkins, a surfer-dude warlock, a vengeful demon, and a Metal Priestess in their way as they try to escape an underground nightmare. **188 pages $13**

BB-029 **"Jesus Freaks" Andre Duza** - For God so loved the world that he gave his only two begotten sons… and a few million zombies. **400 pages $16**

BB-030 **"Grape City" Kevin L. Donihe** - More Donihe-style comedic bizarro about a demon named Charles who is forced to work a minimum wage job on Earth after Hell goes out of business. **108 pages $10**

BB-031**"Sea of the Patchwork Cats" Carlton Mellick III** - A quiet dreamlike tale set in the ashes of the human race. For Mellick enthusiasts who also adore The Twilight Zone. **112 pages $10**

BB-032 **"Extinction Journals" Jeremy Robert Johnson** - An uncanny voyage across a newly nuclear America where one man must confront the problems associated with loneliness, insane dieties, radiation, love, and an ever-evolving cockroach suit with a mind of its own. **104 pages $10**

BB-033 **"Meat Puppet Cabaret" Steve Beard -** At last! The secret connection between Jack the Ripper and Princess Diana's death revealed! **240 pages $16 / $30**

BB-034 **"The Greatest Fucking Moment in Sports" Kevin L. Donihe** - In the tradition of the surreal anti-sitcom Get A Life comes a tale of triumph and agape love from the master of comedic bizarro. **108 pages $10**

BB-035 **"The Troublesome Amputee" John Edward Lawson -** Disturbing verse from a man who truly believes nothing is sacred and intends to prove it. **104 pages $9**

BB-036 **"Deity" Vic Mudd -** God (who doesn't like to be called "God") comes down to a typical, suburban, Ohio family for a little vacation—but it doesn't turn out to be as relaxing as He had hoped it would be... **168 pages $12**

BB-037 **"The Haunted Vagina" Carlton Mellick III -** It's difficult to love a woman whose vagina is a gateway to the world of the dead. **132 pages $10**

BB-038 **"Tales from the Vinegar Wasteland" Ray Fracalossy -** Witness: a man is slowly losing his face, a neighbor who periodically screams out for no apparent reason, and a house with a room that doesn't actually exist. **240 pages $14**

BB-039 **"Suicide Girls in the Afterlife" Gina Ranalli -** After Pogue commits suicide, she unexpectedly finds herself an unwilling "guest" at a hotel in the Afterlife, where she meets a group of bizarre characters, including a goth Satan, a hippie Jesus, and an alien-human hybrid. **100 pages $9**

BB-040 **"And Your Point Is?" Steve Aylett -** In this follow-up to LINT multiple authors provide critical commentary and essays about Jeff Lint's mind-bending literature. **104 pages $11**

BB-041 **"Not Quite One of the Boys" Vincent Sakowski** - While drug-dealer Maxi drinks with Dante in purgatory, God and Satan play a little tri-level chess and do a little bargaining over his business partner, Vinnie, who is still left on earth. **220 pages $14**

BB-042 **"Teeth and Tongue Landscape" Carlton Mellick III** - On a planet made out of meat, a socially-obsessive monophobic man tries to find his place amongst the strange creatures and communities that he comes across. **110 pages $10**

BB-043 **"War Slut" Carlton Mellick III** - Part "1984," part "Waiting for Godot," and part action horror video game adaptation of John Carpenter's "The Thing." **116 pages $10**

BB-044 **"All Encompassing Trip" Nicole Del Sesto** - In a world where coffee is no longer available, the only television shows are reality TV re-runs, and the animals are talking back, Nikki, Amber and a singing Coyote in a do-rag are out to restore the light **308 pages $15**

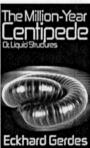

BB-045 **"Dr. Identity" D. Harlan Wilson** - Follow the Dystopian Duo on a killing spree of epic proportions through the irreal postcapitalist city of Bliptown where time ticks sideways, artificial Bug-Eyed Monsters punish citizens for consumer-capitalist lethargy, and ultraviolence is as essential as a daily multivitamin. **208 pages $15**

BB-046 **"The Million-Year Centipede" Eckhard Gerdes** - Wakelin, frontman for 'The Hinge,' wrote a poem so prophetic that to ignore it dooms a person to drown in blood. **130 pages $12**

BB-047 **"Sausagey Santa" Carlton Mellick III** - A bizarro Christmas tale featuring Santa as a piratey mutant with a body made of sausages. 124 pages $10

BB-048 **"Misadventures in a Thumbnail Universe" Vincent Sakowski** - Dive deep into the surreal and satirical realms of neo-classical Blender Fiction, filled with television shoes and flesh-filled skies. **120 pages $10**

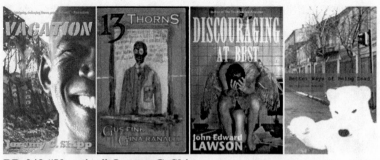

BB-049 **"Vacation" Jeremy C. Shipp** - Blueblood Bernard Johnson leaved his boring life behind to go on The Vacation, a year-long corporate sponsored odyssey. But instead of seeing the world, Bernard is captured by terrorists, becomes a key figure in secret drug wars, and, worse, doesn't once miss his secure American Dream. **160 pages $14**

BB-051 **"13 Thorns" Gina Ranalli** - Thirteen tales of twisted, bizarro horror. **240 pages $13**

BB-050 **"Discouraging at Best" John Edward Lawson** - A collection where the absurdity of the mundane expands exponentially creating a tidal wave that sweeps reason away. For those who enjoy satire, bizarro, or a good old-fashioned slap to the senses. **208 pages $15**

BB-052 **"Better Ways of Being Dead" Christian TeBordo** - In this class, the students have to keep one palm down on the table at all times, and listen to lectures about a panda who speaks Chinese. **216 pages $14**

BB-053 **"Ballad of a Slow Poisoner" Andrew Goldfarb** Millford Mutterwurst sat down on a Tuesday to take his afternoon tea, and made the unpleasant discovery that his elbows were becoming flatter. **128 pages $10**

BB-054 **"Wall of Kiss" Gina Ranalli** - A woman... A wall... Sometimes love blooms in the strangest of places. **108 pages $9**

BB-055 **"HELP! A Bear is Eating Me" Mykle Hansen** - The bizarro, heartwarming, magical tale of poor planning, hubris and severe blood loss... **150 pages $11**

BB-056 **"Piecemeal June" Jordan Krall** - A man falls in love with a living sex doll, but with love comes danger when her creator comes after her with crab-squid assassins. **90 pages $9**

BB-057 **"Laredo" Tony Rauch** - Dreamlike, surreal stories by Tony Rauch. **180 pages $12**

BB-058 **"The Overwhelming Urge" Andersen Prunty** - A collection of bizarro tales by Andersen Prunty. **150 pages $11**

BB-059 **"Adolf in Wonderland" Carlton Mellick III** - A dreamlike adventure that takes a young descendant of Adolf Hitler's design and sends him down the rabbit hole into a world of imperfection and disorder. **180 pages $11**

BB-060 **"Super Cell Anemia" Duncan B. Barlow** - "Unrelentingly bizarre and mysterious, unsettling in all the right ways..." - Brian Evenson. **180 pages $12**

BB-061 **"Ultra Fuckers" Carlton Mellick III** - Absurdist suburban horror about a couple who enter an upper middle class gated community but can't find their way out. **108 pages $9**

BB-062 **"House of Houses" Kevin L. Donihe** - An odd man wants to marry his house. Unfortunately, all of the houses in the world collapse at the same time in the Great House Holocaust. Now he must travel to House Heaven to find his departed fiancee. **172 pages $11**

BB-063 **"Necro Sex Machine" Andre Duza** - The Dead Bitch returns in this follow-up to the bizarro zombie epic Dead Bitch Army. **400 pages $16**

BB-064 **"Squid Pulp Blues" Jordan Krall** - In these three bizarro-noir novellas, the reader is thrown into a world of murderers, drugs made from squid parts, deformed gun-toting veterans, and a mischievous apocalyptic donkey. **204 pages $12**

BB-065 "Jack and Mr. Grin" Andersen Prunty - "When Mr. Grin calls you can hear a smile in his voice. Not a warm and friendly smile, but the kind that seizes your spine in fear. You don't need to pay your phone bill to hear it. That smile is in every line of Prunty's prose." - Tom Bradley. **208 pages $12**

BB-066 "Cybernetrix" Carlton Mellick III - What would you do if your normal everyday world was slowly mutating into the video game world from Tron? **212 pages $12**

BB-067 "Lemur" Tom Bradley - Spencer Sproul is a would-be serial-killing bus boy who can't manage to murder, injure, or even scare anybody. However, there are other ways to do damage to far more people and do it legally... **120 pages $12**

BB-068 "Cocoon of Terror" Jason Earls - Decapitated corpses...a sculpture of terror...Zelian's masterpiece, his Cocoon of Terror, will trigger a supernatural disaster for everyone on Earth. **196 pages $14**

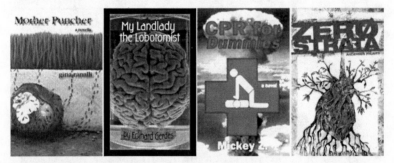

BB-069 "Mother Puncher" Gina Ranalli - The world has become tragically over-populated and now the government strongly opposes procreation. Ed is employed by the government as a mother-puncher. He doesn't relish his job, but he knows it has to be done and he knows he's the best one to do it. **120 pages $9**

BB-070 "My Landlady the Lobotomist" Eckhard Gerdes - The brains of past tenants line the shelves of my boarding house, soaking in a mysterious elixir. One more slip-up and the landlady might just add my frontal lobe to her collection. **116 pages $12**

BB-071 "CPR for Dummies" Mickey Z. - This hilarious freakshow at the world's end is the fragmented, sobering debut novel by acclaimed nonfiction author Mickey Z. **216 pages $14**

BB-072 "Zerostrata" Andersen Prunty - Hansel Nothing lives in a tree house, suffers from memory loss, has a very eccentric family, and falls in love with a woman who runs naked through the woods every night. **144 pages $11**

BB-073 **"The Egg Man" Carlton Mellick III** - It is a world where humans reproduce like insects. Children are the property of corporations, and having an enormous ten-foot brain implanted into your skull is a grotesque sexual fetish. Mellick's industrial urban dystopia is one of his darkest and grittiest to date. **184 pages $11**

BB-074 **"Shark Hunting in Paradise Garden" Cameron Pierce** - A group of strange humanoid religious fanatics travel back in time to the Garden of Eden to discover it is invested with hundreds of giant flying maneating sharks. **150 pages $10**

BB-075 **"Apeshit" Carlton Mellick III** - Friday the 13th meets Visitor Q. Six hipster teens go to a cabin in the woods inhabited by a deformed killer. An incredibly fucked-up parody of B-horror movies with a bizarro slant. **192 pages $12**

BB-076 **"Rampaging Fuckers of Everything on the Crazy Shitting Planet of the Vomit At smosphere" Mykle Hansen** - 3 bizarro satires. Monster Cocks, Journey to the Center of Agnes Cuddlebottom, and Crazy Shitting Planet. **228 pages $12**

BB-077 **"The Kissing Bug" Daniel Scott Buck** - In the tradition of Roald Dahl, Tim Burton, and Edward Gorey, comes this bizarro anti-war children's story about a bohemian conenose kissing bug who falls in love with a human woman. **116 pages $10**

BB-078 **"MachoPoni" Lotus Rose** - It's My Little Pony... *Bizarro* style! A long time ago Poniworld was split in two. On one side of the Jagged Line is the Pastel Kingdom, a magical land of music, parties, and positivity. On the other side of the Jagged Line is Dark Kingdom inhabited by an army of undead ponies. **148 pages $11**

BB-079 **"The Faggiest Vampire" Carlton Mellick III** - A Roald Dahl-esque children's story about two faggy vampires who partake in a mustache competition to find out which one is truly the faggiest. **104 pages $10**

BB-080 **"Sky Tongues" Gina Ranalli** - The autobiography of Sky Tongues, the biracial hermaphrodite actress with tongues for fingers. Follow her strange life story as she rises from freak to fame. **204 pages $12**

BB-081 **"Washer Mouth" Kevin L. Donihe** - A washing machine becomes human and pursues his dream of meeting his favorite soap opera star. **244 pages $11**

BB-082 **"Shatnerquake" Jeff Burk** - All of the characters ever played by William Shatner are suddenly sucked into our world. Their mission: hunt down and destroy the real William Shatner. **100 pages $10**

BB-083 **"The Cannibals of Candyland" Carlton Mellick III** - There exists a race of cannibals that are made of candy. They live in an underground world made out of candy. One man has dedicated his life to killing them all. **170 pages $11**

BB-084 **"Slub Glub in the Weird World of the Weeping Willows" Andrew Goldfarb** - The charming tale of a blue glob named Slub Glub who helps the weeping willows whose tears are flooding the earth. There are also hyenas, ghosts, and a voodoo priest **100 pages $10**

BB-085 **"Super Fetus" Adam Pepper** - Try to abort this fetus and he'll kick your ass! **104 pages $10**

BB-086 **"Fistful of Feet" Jordan Krall** - A bizarro tribute to spaghetti westerns, featuring Cthulhu-worshipping Indians, a woman with four feet, a crazed gunman who is obsessed with sucking on candy, Syphilis-ridden mutants, sexually transmitted tattoos, and a house devoted to the freakiest fetishes. **228 pages $12**

BB-087 **"Ass Goblins of Auschwitz" Cameron Pierce** - It's Monty Python meets Nazi exploitation in a surreal nightmare as can only be imagined by Bizarro author Cameron Pierce. **104 pages $10**

BB-088 **"Silent Weapons for Quiet Wars" Cody Goodfellow** - "This is high-end psychological surrealist horror meets bottom-feeding low-life crime in a techno-thrilling science fiction world full of Lovecraft and magic..." -John Skipp **212 pages $12**

ORDER FORM

TITLES	QTY	PRICE	TOTAL

Please make checks and moneyorders payable to ROSE O'KEEFE / BIZARRO BOOKS in U.S. funds only. Please don't send bad checks! Allow 2-6 weeks for delivery. International orders may take longer. If you'd like to pay online via PAYPAL.COM, send payments to publisher@eraserheadpress.com.

SHIPPING: US ORDERS - $2 for the first book, $1 for each additional book. For priority shipping, add an additional $4. INT'L ORDERS - $5 for the first book, $3 for each additional book. Add an additional $5 per book for global priority shipping.

Send payment to:

BIZARRO BOOKS
C/O Rose O'Keefe
205 NE Bryant
Portland, OR 97211

Address		
City	State	Zip
Email	Phone	

CPSIA information can be obtained at www.ICGtesting.com
Printed in the USA
LVOW070905020112

261879LV00001B/206/P